COPYRIGHT ACKNOWLEDGEMENTS

"Fireflies"—originally published in *Polluto #9*. Selected as an honorable mention by Ellen Datlow for *Best Horror of the Year*

"Chrysalis"—originally published in *Arcadia #6*

"Love Letters"—originally published in *Cannoli Pie #12*

"Vision Quest"—originally published in Surreal Grotesque #1

"Surrender"—originally published in the *Booked* anthology by Booked Podcast

"The Wastelands"—originally published in the *Into the Darkness* anthology from Necro Publications

"Misty"—originally published at *ManArchy Magazine*

"The Handyman"—originally published in *Conjectural Figments #1*

"Bringing in the Sheaves"—originally published at *Beat the Dust*

"Divining"—originally published in *Curbside Splendor #3*

"The Culling"—originally published in *Fear the Reaper*, from Crystal Lake Publishing

"Flowers for Jessica"—originally published in *Weird Fiction Review #3* from Centipede Press

"Wicker Park Pause"—originally published in *One Buck Horror #5*, winner of the Café Doom / One Buck Horror short story contest

"On a Bent Nail Head"—originally published in the *Nova Parade* anthology from Solarcide

"Dance, Darling"—originally published in the *Cipher Sisters* anthology from Thunderdome Press

"The Fix-It Man"—originally published at *Black Heart Magazine*

"Gandaberunda"—originally published at *ManArchy Magazine*

"Shackled to the Shadows"—originally published in the *Truth or Dare?* anthology, from Perpetual Motion Machine Publishing

"Playing with Fire"—originally published in the *Chiral Mad 2* anthology, from Written Backwards

"Little Red Wagon"—originally published in *Litro Magazine*

"Asking for Forgiveness"—originally published at *Menacing Hedge, Issue 4.01*

"Balance Sheet"—originally published in *Penumbra Magazine*, Volume 3, Issue 11

"White Picket Fences"—originally published in the *Shadows Over Main Street* anthology from Hazardous Press

"Chasing Ghosts"—originally published in *Cemetery Dance #72*

"The Offering on the Hill"—originally published in *Chiral Mad 3*, published by Written Backwards

CONTENTS

EPIGRAPH

" . . . a short story is like a kiss in the dark from a stranger."

—Stephen King, *Skeleton Crew*

"Old stories would tell how Weavers would kill each other over aesthetic disagreements, such as whether it was prettier to destroy an army of a thousand men or to leave it be, or whether a particular dandelion should or should not be plucked. For a Weaver, to think was to think aesthetically. To act—to Weave—was to bring about more pleasing patterns. They did not eat physical food: they seemed to subsist on the appreciation of beauty."

—China Miéville, *Perdido Street Station*

"Tell me, Doctor, are you afraid of death?"
"I guess it depends on how you die."

—Haruki Murakami, *The Wind-Up Bird Chronicle*

DEDICATION

That part of your writing that scares you, that doesn't fit neatly into any one genre, that's a little weird? I want more of that. That's your voice. This is mine. I dedicate this book to anyone who has ever been called weird, strange, unusual, a freak—whatever. You know the opposite of those words? Normal, average, common—and who wants that? Not me.

INTRODUCTION

A GOOD COLLECTION of horror stories will, at two in the morning, direct your car more to Motel 6 than Super 8, say. Just because you want to be in a room where someone's left the light on for you.

Tribulations does that for you, yes? Or, Richard Thomas is doing that for Motel 6.

Either way, it's delivering the creepy visuals, the prose that worms into your head and crawls around on the backside of your skull.

And we ask for that, don't we?

We stand at the register and we lay down our money, fully expecting to not be able to turn the lights off that night.

But that's just what we expect from our horror. That's the minimum horror has to do to satisfy.

A really good collection of horror stories, then—like this one you're holding in your hands—it does that and it provides something else, something even creepier and crawlier, something wormier and altogether less comfortable. Something you wouldn't necessarily ask for.

A really good collection of horror stories can give us a glimpse into the writer's head. Reading Tribulations, a story or two in, you're thinking this is normal, this is what I paid for, bring it, Thomas.

But then.

There'll be an image or a construction that seeps up to the surface for the second or second-and-a-half time, and you'll look away from the page, trying to recall exactly where this happened before.

In something else you were reading?

No, no—it was just a few minutes ago, wasn't it?

It was here.

And then you read for another little bit, get drawn in by the pacing, by the tension, by the language—Richard Thomas knows his craft, has good instincts—and it happens again: you've recognized a girl, say. Not her specifically, but the way she's described—"described" isn't even the right word for this. It's the way the light of the story is shining on her. It's her shadow on the wall.

That's a shadow Tribulations has been fascinated with for a while, now.

But that's not right either.

That's a girl Richard Thomas can't seem to look away from. What it comes to feel like is a corruption in him, that he's trying to infect us with, so as to save himself.

You don't come to expect this in every horror collection. Too many of them are just Greatest Hits. Too many are just the writer standing in the story closet, trying on the vampire jacket, the mummy glasses, the ghost shoes.

A strong horror collection, though, it has a purpose. It's the writer trying to unburden him or herself of something corrupt, something not so much with teeth but with arms that reach around from behind to caress you, to pull you back into itself and

INTRODUCTION

whisper into your ears for the rest of however long you've got.

And, how long you've got, it's not long, it's never long.

Although, it can feel a lot like forever.

So, read this if you dare, read it with gloves on, with protective eye gear, with your mind encased in mental plastic.

It won't matter.

There's something corrupt here.

And she's watching us from between these lines.

Be careful.

Stephen Graham Jones
Salt Lake City,
September 2015

FIREFLIES

WHEN THE WINDS come, the hut shakes and I grab the tabletop, the heavy wood carved centuries ago, scarred and pitted by time. I wait for the roof to rip off, exposing me to some giant hand, pulling me into the sky to be punished for my sins. The beams creak and moan, and in the gaps I hear her voice. I beg her to shut up, to leave me alone, but the dull ache that wraps around my plodding heart, it trembles and hesitates, apologizes for snapping at her, my love, and asks her for forgiveness. And she gives it, freely.

The scrap of paper dances in the wooden bowl, the printed type from another time, so long ago, when machines still ruled the world. It nestles into the handful of buckeyes, their dull red orbs rolling around—a fluttering eagle feather next to the pink fleshy lining of an aging conch shell. I've memorized the serial number that runs along the bottom, the bent edges of the stained slip, once a shiny white stock, now a dull, faded yellow. The solitary word used to make me laugh. Isabella and I would dance in their glow, mocking the insects, asking them to take us home—to smother us in their amber. I don't laugh about them anymore.

After the winds start up it isn't long until the black rain beats down upon the tin roof, sheets of metal scraps stolen from ruptured airplanes that dot the island, bent and fastened by my tired, mangled hands. When the door swings open, I'm not surprised—the latch has been busted for days now, and my hope was that it would fix itself, the wood warped and swollen, praying for the doorframe to shift back to its former self. Shadows drift in from the field, lightning fracturing the night. The long grass bends, rippling in the flash of light, photos taken as her arms raise and lower, long legs extended, leaping, and I shake my head, squint my eyes shut, and beg for more time. Not tonight. I'm too fragile to handle the haunting.

And then it is quiet. She is gone, my memory of her body, her giving curves and gentle fingers fading into the night. Beyond the field lies the edge of the cliff, and beyond that is the water of a never ending ocean, black as tar, a universe expanding, calling me to take the long swim home.

At the edges there is a history, a blur of wagons and horses, bodies piled high, the stench taking on a physical weight, splintered doors slamming shut like gunshots as the dead were taken away. She was taken away, and for nothing more than a ripe peach hanging from an abandoned tree, the orchard ripe with flies and decaying nectar. But the disease had taken hold already, whatever we called the mutation then, the plague had come home to roost, to rest—to unfold.

"Isabella," I sigh, a wave of moonlight crossing the field, crawling over the lush grass, wandering inside the hut. I light the candles that sit in a melted pile, now that the winds have died down. The box of matches is running low, a trip to the town square near at hand.

The howling will start soon, the rabid pack of mongrels coming to sniff at the cracks of my homestead, licking at the sap that plugs the gaps, snuffling at the door, rattling the frame with their dark, wet snouts, pissing on it and moving on in a sickening mass of dark, hairy flesh. There is little time to fix the latch, but I must.

On the wall hang a few handmade instruments— bent metal and wood stained with the slick oil of my flesh. I am not a blacksmith nor am I a carpenter. These tools are about all I have. Heavy rocks work just as well and sometimes I get lucky in the wreckage, a steel beam or bar changing the way that my life staggers on. So many times I've frayed the flesh of my fingers just to steal a bolt or two, a handful of nuts and nails taken from the bent and empty metal birds. And to what end? In a few days when I'm drained by the sunlight that beats down on this solitary rock, the heat will push me down until I collapse in the sand on the east side of the island, seashells spilling from my hands. Or the exhaustion will leave me in the meadow, covered in tiny cuts from the sharp blades of grass that surround me, lost to time and place. The black winged beasts will descend on my homestead, pecking at the shiny objects, these diseased children of the raven and magpie. The dogs will take what is left, I don't know why, scattering the bits of metal far and wide, the dull pieces of steel picked up by the deformed rodents that live in the caves down by the water. They mock me. But I continue. She tells me to carry on.

I take down the bastard screwdriver and

malformed hammer and push at the lock that protrudes from the door, trying to straighten it out, to solidify this pitiful lock, so that the demon beasts will not get in tonight.

The wind picks up again as I crouch in the doorway, the coolness washing over my slick skin, and the grass waves back and forth, telling me to come lay down in the damp finery of their offerings, and for a moment, I stop and consider doing just that.

No. The latch.

I lick my lips and bend the piece of metal, the rusted tongue eluding my clumsy fingers, the metal in my hand slipping, running a gash through my left hand. I shove my palm into my mouth, cursing as I sup the liquid, knowing that it will surely draw them out. And at the edge of the field there is a flickering of lights, dots of yellow fading in and out—they've smelled the humanity that drips onto the stone porch, the slab of grey rock dotted with discs of red and I hurry to bend the metal straight.

To my left the glowing circles meander across the night sky, taking their time. They have all night to play with me and I have nowhere to go. My eyes stay on them, watching as they pulse in and out, slowly moving across the field, the cool metal in my hands finally bending. I check my work, lifting the latch up and down, my eyes drawn back to the field and to my handiwork. I step inside and close the door, their night music fading behind the dense wood. Sliding the lock in place, I tug on the brass knob and it holds, it is solid, and the shadows pour over the edge of the cliff, stretching and shrinking, eager to test my work. I rattle the knob one more time.

FIREFLIES

I sit down at the table, the old wooden chair creaking under my weight, as the panic drains out of my skin, my face falling into my open hands, muffling a sob that has been building all day.

"Oh, Isabelle," I moan. "Help me, my love."

I can hear them circling the house, their hot rancid breath coming out in gasps, the wet lapping of their tongues in the air, teeth clicking, snapping at each other as their hackles raise and a heavy wind pushes against the house. I don't want to blow out the candles—they give me comfort and warmth. I've only just lit them with my dwindling supply of matches—but I do it anyway.

"Go away," I yell, and they yip and bark, excited by my anger, hoping to lure me outside, wanting the confrontation—willing me to take them on tonight. I hear a clang of metal on the slab outside and creep over to look between the cracks. A body slams against the door and I fall backward, my heart stuttering, a long bit of rusted rebar lying on the rock like a sacrifice. I smile against all logic. I grin in the darkness despite my need to piss, my stomach rolling and unfurling—they want me to take this weapon, they're trying to even up the odds. Manipulative bastards.

Another heavy weight is flung against the door and I worry the latch will not hold. There is a sharp cry and the furry beasts move away from the front of the hut, and I hear the animals disappear behind the house. A gathering of yellow lights hovers in front of the door, and this may be my only chance tonight. I flick the metal latch up and step forward, flipping my head to the left and then the right, the wind gusting, grasses sighing, and I bend over to pick up the bar. The glowing dots gather before me and I stand upright as they fill the frame of my Isabella, just for a moment, her curves and slender legs, her long hair blowing in the darkness, and then they break apart. I take a step outside.

The fireflies head back across the grassy field, a line of yellow dots, expanding into slashes, and I follow this lost highway out into the night, a wave of peaceful inevitability washing over me, the hounds coming back around to the front, yapping at me, nipping at my feet, my knees, as they bound in and out of the grasses. I swing the bar lazily toward them, and they retreat. Moments later they are back at my side, escorting me through the lapping blades. I fling the bar out into the grass and it lands with a dull thud, the animals descending on it, confused. They sniff at the metal, something off, standing still now, and they let me continue, rotting flesh that I am—they let me go.

When the blinking lights drift out over the water and up into the sky, I follow them. She whispers in my ear, her mouth on my neck, and the tears come, the dancing lights pulling me over. Her laughter is with me and I take it, I hold it, and let it cushion me as I fall to embrace the rocks below.

CHRYSALIS

JOHN REDMAN STOOD in his living room, the soft glow of the embers in the fireplace casting his shadow against the wall, and wondered how much he could get if he returned all of the gifts that were under the Christmas tree—everything—including what was in the stockings. The wind picked up outside the old farmhouse, rattling a loose piece of wood trim, the windows shaking, a cool draft of air settling on his skin. Couple hundred bucks maybe, four hundred tops. But it might be enough. That paired with their savings, everything that his wife Laura and he had in the bank—the paltry sum of maybe six hundred dollars. It had to be done. Every ache in his bones, every day that passed—a little more panic settled down onto shoulders, the weight soon becoming unbearable. Upstairs the kids were asleep, Jed and Missy quiet in their beds, home from school for their winter break, filling up the house with their warm laughter and vigilante footsteps. Everything that went back, the long drive to the city, miles and miles of desolate farmland his only escort, it pained him to consider it at all. Video games and dolls, new jeans and sweaters, and a single diamond on a locket hung from a long strand of silver. All of it was going back.

RICHARD THOMAS

It had started a couple weeks ago with, of all things, a large orange and black wooly bear caterpillar. He stood on the back porch sneaking a cigarette, his wife and kids in town, grocery shopping and running errands all day. The fuzzy beast crawled across the porch rail and stopped right next to John—making sure it was seen. John looked at the caterpillar and noticed it was almost completely black, with just a tiny band of orange. Something in that information rang a bell, shot up a red flag in the back of his crowded mind. He usually didn't pay attention to these kinds of things— give them any weight. Sure, he picked up his Farmer's Almanac every year, partly out of habit, and partly because it all made him laugh. Owning the farm as they did now, seven years or so, taking over for his mother when she passed away, the children still infants, unable to complain, John had gotten a lot of advice. Every time he stepped into Clancy's Dry Goods in town, picking up his contraband cigarettes, or a six-pack of Snickers bars that he hid in the glove box of his faded red pickup truck, the advice spilled out of his elder's mouths like the dribble that used to run down his children's chins. Clancy himself told John to make sure he picked up the almanac, to get his woodpile in order, to put up plastic over the windows, in preparation for winter. For some reason, John listened to the barrel-chested man, his moustache and goatee giving him an air of sophistication that was offset by Clancy's fondness for flannel. John nodded his head when the Caterpillar and John Deere hats jawed on and on by the coffeepot, stomping their boots to shake off the cold, rubbing their hands over three-day old stubble. John nodded his head and went out the door, usually snickering to himself.

CHRYSALIS

Christmas was coming and the three-bedroom farmhouse was filled with the smell of oranges and cloves, hot apple cider, and a large brick fireplace that was constantly burning, night and day. Laura taught English at the high school, and she was off work as well. Most of the month of December and a little bit of the new year would unfurl to fill their home with crayons, fresh baked bread, and Matchbox cars laid out in rows and sorted by color.

John was an accountant, a CPA. He'd taken over his father's business, Comprehensive Accounting, a few years before they'd finally made the move to the farm. The client list was set, most every small business in the area, and a few of the bigger ones as well. They trusted John with their business, the only history that mattered to them were the new ones he created with their books. Every year he balanced the accounts, hiding numbers over here, padding expenses over there, working his magic, his illusion. But Laura knew John better, back before the children were born, back when their evenings were filled with broken glasses and lipstick stains and money gambled away on lies and risky ventures. Things were good now—John was on a short leash, nowhere to go, miles from everyone— trouble pushed away and sent on down the road.

John made a mental note of the caterpillar, to look it up later in the almanac. Right now he had wood to chop, stocking up for the oncoming season. He tugged on his soft, leather gloves, stained with sap and soil, faded and fraying at the edges. Surrounding the farmhouse was a ring of trees, oak and maple and evergreen pine. For miles in every direction there were fields of amber, corn on one side—soybeans on the other. John picked up the axe that leaned against the back porch with his left hand, and then grabbed the chainsaw with his right—eyeballing the caterpillar, which hadn't moved an inch, as he walked forward exhaling white puffs of air. One day the fields were a comfort, the fact that they leased them out to local farmers, no longer actual farmers themselves, a box checked in the appropriate column, incoming funds— an asset. The next day they closed in on him, their watchful stare a constant presence, a reminder of something he was not—reliable.

John set the axe and chainsaw next to a massive oak and looked around the ring of trees. There were small branches scattered under the trees—he picked these up in armloads and took them back to the house, filling a large box with the bits of wood. This would be the kindling. Then he went back to look for downed trees—smaller ones mostly, their roots unable to stand up to the winds that whipped across the open plains and bent the larger trees back and forth. A fog pushed in across the open land, thick and heavy, blanketing the ring of trees, filling in all the gaps. The ground was covered in acorns, a blanket of caps and nuts, nowhere to step that didn't end in pops and cracks, his boot rolling across the tiny orbs.

"Damn. When did these all fall down? Overnight?"

John stared up into the arms of the oak trees, spider webs spanning their open arms, stretching across the gaps, thick and white—floating in the breeze. He looked to the other trees and saw acorns scattered beneath them all, and more spider webs high up into the foliage. Spying a downed tree, he left the axe alone for now and picked up the chainsaw, tugging

CHRYSALIS

on the string, the bark and buzz filling the yard with angry noise.

Several hours later the cord of wood was stacked against the side of the house, the tree sectioned down into manageable logs, which were then split in half, and then halved again. It was a solid yield, probably enough to get them through the winter—the box of kindling overflowing with twigs and branches that had been broken over his knee. They would keep an eye on the backyard, and over the course of the winter, they would refill the box with the fallen branches and twigs. The winds picked up again as John took a breath, a sheen of sweat on the back of his neck, night settling in around the farm.

When he finally went inside, the wife and kids home from their errands, the house smelled of freshly baked cookies, chocolate chip, if John knew his wife. The kids were up on barstools around the butcher block island, hands covered in flour, their faces dotted with white, his wife at the kitchen sink washing dishes. In the corner of the window was a singular ladybug, red and dotted with black.

"Daddy," Missy yelled, hopping down off her stool. She ran over to him, painting his jeans with tiny, white handprints.

"Hey, pumpkin," John said. "Cookies?"

"Chocolate chip," she beamed.

"Jed, could you get me a glass of water?" John asked. His son didn't answer, concentrating on the cookie dough. "Jed. Water?" His son didn't answer.

"I'll get it, Daddy," Missy said.

"No, honey, I want Jed to get it. I know he can hear me."

John lowered his voice to a whisper, his eyes on Jed the whole time. "I'm going to count to three," John hissed, his daughter's eyes squinting, her head lowering as she crept out of the way. "Get me that water, boy, or you'll be picking out a switch." Jed didn't move, a smile starting to turn up his mouth, the cookie dough still in his hands."

"Daddy?" Missy said, her face scrunching up. "He doesn't hear you, don't . . . "

"Honey, go," John continued. "One," John peeled off his gloves and dropped them by the back door. "Two," he whispered, unbuttoning his coat, pulling his hat off and dropping it on the floor. He inhaled for three, a thin needle pushing through his heart, this constant battle that he had with his son, the grade school maturation placing in front of John a new hurdle every day. The boy got off the stool, leaving behind the cookies, and tugged on the back of his mother's apron strings.

"Mom, can I get a glass of water for Dad, please?"

Laura stopped doing the dishes, her long brown ponytail swishing to one side as she turned to look at the boy. She handed him a tall glass and pointed him to the refrigerator. Off he went to get the water and ice, pushing the glass against the built-in dispenser, a modern day convenience they all enjoyed. Jed walked over to his dad and held the glass out to him, eyes glued to his father's belt buckle.

"Jed?"

"Yes, Dad?" he said, looking up, brown eyes pooled and distant.

"Thank you," John said, leaning over, hugging the boy. The little man leaned into his father. "Thanks for the water," John said, kissing the boy on the cheek. It just took a little more work, that's all.

Later that night, John sat in his study, while Laura put the kids to bed. He thumbed through the almanac, looking at the index, studying the upcoming months, the forecast for the Midwestern winter. There were several things that got his attention. When the forecast was for a particularly bad winter, harsh conditions to come, there were signs and warnings everywhere. For example, if a wooly bear caterpillar was mostly orange, then the winter coming up would be mild. His caterpillar had almost no orange at all. He kept looking for other signs. If there is an inordinate amount of fog, if there are a lot of spider webs, especially high up in the corners of houses, barns or trees—the bigger the webs, the worse the winter. If pine trees are extra bushy; if there are halos around the sun or the moon; if there are a lot of acorns on the ground—these are the signs of a rough winter to come—rumors, and legends, and lore.

John closed the book and set it down, a chill settling in across his spine. A draft slipped through the study window, the plastic sheets he'd meant to put up, forgotten. It was nothing. The stupid almanac was a bunch of crap, he thought. He stood up and went down to the basement anyway.

Along one wall were several wooden shelves—he'd built them himself when they moved in. There were jars of preserves and jam, jellies and fruit, all along the top shelf. Further down, on the second shelf were soups and vegetables and other canned goods. It was almost empty, maybe a dozen cans of diced tomatoes and chicken noodle soup. On the third shelf were boxed goods, everything from pasta to scalloped potatoes to rice. It was fairly packed, so he moved on to the second set of shelves. It was filled with family-sized packages of toilet paper and paper towels, napkins and cleaning supplies. Then, he turned to the ancient furnace and stared.

Settled into the center of the room was the original furnace that came with the house. Built in the late 1800s, the farmhouse came equipped with a coal chute that opened up on the back of the house. Concrete poured into the ground at an angle, stopped at thick, metal doors—which if pulled open revealed the long abandoned chute that ran down to the basement floor. It was a novelty, really—historic and breathtaking to look at, but nothing more than a pile of greasy metal. The massive, black ironworks dwarfed the modern water heater and fans, doors slotted like a set of enormous teeth, squatting in the middle of the room. Maybe he'd talk to Clancy.

It was fifteen miles to the nearest big city and the large chain grocery stores. John simply drove in to town. Clancy was about the same price, a couple cents higher here and there. But he felt better putting his money in the hands of a friend than a faceless corporation.

He felt stupid pushing the miniature grocery cart around the store. A flush of red ran up his neck as he bought every can of soup that Clancy had.

"Jesus, man," Clancy said, as John brought the

cart up to the counter. "You done bought up all my soup."

"Order more," John said.

"I guess so," Clancy said, ringing him up.

"Can I ask you something?" John said.

"Shoot, brother. What's on your mind?"

"That furnace we have out at the farm, the old one? Does it work?"

"Well, let me think. It's still hooked up to the vents as far as I know. The little valves are closed off, is all— easy to flip them open. Helped your dad out with some ductwork a long time ago, he showed me how it all went together. But, you'd have to have a shitload of coal. And I have no idea of where you'd get that, these days. Does anyone still burn it?"

John nodded his head. He knew where he could get some coal. But it wasn't cheap, that's for sure.

"Just curious," John said. "How much are those gallons of water, by the way," John asked, pointing at a dusty display at the front of the store. There were maybe two-dozen gallons of water.

"Those are .89 cents a gallon, can't seem to move them."

"I'll take them," John said.

"How many?" Clancy asked.

"All of them."

John was supposed to be down at his office. Instead, the back of his pickup truck was loaded up with soup and water, and he was headed down to the river. About two miles east, a small branch of the Mississippi wormed its way out into the land. A buddy of his from high school had a loading dock out there. Sometimes it was just people hopping on there in canoes, or boats, paddling down to the main branch of the river, or just buzzing up and down the water. Other times it was barges, loaded up with corn or soybeans—and sometimes coal from down south. There was a power plant upstate from where they lived, and it burned off a great deal of coal. Sometimes it was a train that passed by the plant, offloading great cars of the black mineral. And sometimes there were barges, drifting up the water, shimmering in the moonlight.

John pulled up to the trailer and hopped out. It was getting colder. He looked up at the cloudy sky, a soft halo wrapping around the sun, hiding behind the clouds. All around the tiny trailer were evergreen trees, fat and bushy, creeping in close to the metal structure, huddled up for warmth.

John knocked on the trailer door.

"Come in," a voice bellowed.

John stepped into the trailer, which was filled with smoke.

"Damn, Jamie, do you ever stop smoking? Open a window, why don't you."

"Well, hello to you too, John. Welcome to my humble abode. What brings you out here?"

John sat down and stared at his old buddy. Jamie was never going anywhere. Born and raised here in the northern part of the heartland, this was it for him. And it seemed to suit him just fine. No college, no aspirations, no dreams of the big city—happy to live and die where he was born.

"Coal," John said. "I'm just wondering. You sell it to people?"

CHRYSALIS

"Not usually. Got a few guys with old pot bellied stoves off in the woods. They buy a sack off of me, now and then. You know, I just kind of skim it off the top, the electric company none the wiser."

"How much does it cost?"

"Depends. One guy I charge $20 because he's broke and has a hot sister. Other guy is a jerk, and his sister's a hag. I charge him $50. I could cut you a deal though, John. Happy to help out an old friend."

"What about a larger quantity"

"How much we talking about, John?"

"Like, filling up my pickup truck?" John said.

Jamie whistled and tapped his fingertips on his mouth. "That's trouble. Can't skim that. Have to pay full price, actually talk to the barge man. Unload it. Not even sure when the next shipment will be rolling through. Getting cold."

John shivered. "If you had to guess though, any idea?"

Jamie took a breath. "Maybe a grand."

⌒

John drove home, almost dark now, his house still miles away. When he pulled up the driveway, the tires rolling over more acorns, the house was dark. Where the hell were they? He pulled up to the back of the house, and hurried to unload the truck. Into the kitchen he went, armloads of soup cans, hurrying to get them downstairs. Why was he sweating so much, why did this feel like a secret? He dropped a can of tomato soup but kept on going. He loaded the soups on the second shelf and went back for more. Two trips, three trips, and the dozens of cans of soup filled up the shelf with a weight that calmed him down. Back upstairs he picked up the can he'd dropped and looked out the window to see if they were home yet. A handful of ladybugs were scattered across the glass, and he scrunched up his nose at their presence.

Back to the truck, a gallon of water in each hand, this was going to take a little while. The soup he could explain—an impulse buy, Clancy running some kind of stupid sale: buy a can of soup get a stick of homemade jerky for free. But the two-dozen gallons of water looked like panic. He didn't want them to worry, even as he contemplated the coal, the thing he may have to do in secret, the risk he'd have to take. Up and down the steps he went, pushing the water to the back of the basement, covering it up with a stained and flecked drop cloth. He stared at the canned goods, the water, and the coal powered furnace. A door slammed upstairs, and his head turned.

The kids were yelling for him, so he pulled the string that clicked off the light, and back upstairs he went.

"Hey, honey," he said. "What's up, guys?"

The kids gave him a quick hug and then ran on to their rooms. Laura leaned into him, looking tired, and gave him a kiss on the lips.

"You smell like smoke," she said. "You smoking again?" she asked.

"Nah. Saw an old friend. Jamie, you remember him? Chain smokes like a fiend."

Laura eyeballed John.

"Why are you all sweaty?"

"Just putting some stuff away, couple trips up and down the stairs, no big deal."

Laura puckered her lips, swallowed and moved to the sink. She turned on the water and washed off her hands.

"Why don't you go take a shower and get cleaned up? You stink. Dinner will be ready soon."

Later that night John watched the news, Laura in the kitchen doing the dishes. The weatherman laid out the forecast all the way up to Christmas and beyond. Cold. It was dipping down, probably into the teens. Snow. A few inches here and there, but nothing to cause any alarm. He switched over to another station, the same thing. He tried the Weather Channel, watching the whole country, the Midwest especially, storm fronts rolling down from Canada, but nothing to worry about.

"How much weather do you need, hon?" Laura said, sticking her head in from the kitchen. "You've been watching that for like an hour."

"Oh," he said. "I was just spacing out, wasn't really watching it. You wanna sit down and watch something with me?"

"Sure. Want some tea?"

John got up and walked into the kitchen, Laura's back still to him, and wrapped his arms around her waist. She relaxed into his arms, and leaned back. He kissed her on the neck, holding her tight, his mouth moving up to her ear lobe, where he licked and nibbled at her gently.

"Or, we could just go up to bed early," she smiled.

"We could do that," he said.

Behind her on the window there were several dozen ladybugs now, bunched up in the corner, a tiny, vibrating hive—and beyond that a slowly expanding moon with a ghost of a halo running around it.

The next day they woke up to snow, three inches on the ground, heavy flakes falling like a sheet, white for as far as he could see. The kids were screaming, laughing, excited to get out into it, his wife calming them down with requests to eat, to sit still, to wait. For John the snowfall made his stomach clench, the way the tiny icicles hung from the gutters, the pile of dead ladybugs covering the windowsill, the sense that he had blown it, missed his opportunity—the claustrophobia closing in.

All day John walked around with his temples throbbing, trembling gut in turmoil—his mouth dry and filled with cotton. To keep his hands busy he pulled a roll of plastic out of the garage, and sealed up every window in the house. When the sun came out and melted everything away, the children were disappointed.

John was not.

When Laura fell asleep on the couch, the kids watching cartoons, John made a call to Jamie. Three days for the coal, the day before Christmas, still a thousand dollars for the weight. If the weather held, it gave him time. He told Jamie to make it happen. He'd have it for him in cash.

The afternoon couldn't pass fast enough, Laura constantly staring at him from across the room. He cleaned up the dead ladybugs, then went downstairs and placed a cardboard box on the tarp that sat on the water, trying to hide his anxiety with a plastic smile.

The middle of the night was his only chance, so he

crept downstairs with his pocketknife in his robe pocket, and slit open the presents one by one. He peeled back the tape gently, no tearing allowed, and emptied the presents from their wrappings. Where he could, he left the cardboard boxes empty for now and prayed that nobody shook the presents. For others, he wrapped up new shapes, empty boxes he found stacked down the basement. Grabbing a large black trash bag from under the sink he filled it up with clothing and gifts, the tiny jewelry box going into his pocket. When he was done, he opened the cookie jar, the green grouch that sat up high on one of the shelves. He pulled out the receipts and stuffed them in his pocket, and slunk out to the truck to hide the loot.

When he stepped back into the kitchen Laura was standing there, arms crossed, watching him.

"Dammit, Laura, you scared me."

"What the hell are you doing, John?"

"Taking out the trash."

"At three in the morning?" she asked. She walked over and sniffed him.

"You know," he said, smiling. "Christmas is only a couple days away. Maybe you don't want to look so close at what I'm doing. Maybe there are surprises for wives that don't snoop too hard," John said.

Laura grinned and held out her hand.

"Come to bed," she said.

Out the window the full moon carried a ring that shone across the night.

⌇

John got up early and left a note. It was the best way

to get out of the house without any questions. He left his wife and kids sleeping, and snuck out the back door, the wind whipping his jacket open, mussing his hair, bending the trees back and forth.

All day he drove, one place to the next, his stories changing, his stories remaining the same. Too large, too small; changed my mind, she already has one; got the wrong one, my kids are so damn picky. The wad of bills in his pocket got thicker. The pain behind his eyes spread across his skull.

What was he doing?

He stopped by the bank, the day before Christmas now, and cleared out their checking and savings, leaving only enough to keep the accounts open. He took his thousand dollars and drove out to the trailer, Jamie sitting there as if he hadn't moved.

"All there?" Jamie asked, leaning back in his chair.

"To the nickel."

"Tomorrow night then," Jamie said. "Christmas Eve."

"Yep."

"What the hell are you doing, John," Jamie asked.

"The only thing I can."

When John got home Laura rushed out to the car.

"The fireplace," she said, "It's caved in."

John looked up to the tall brickwork that was now leaning to one side, the winds whipping up a tornado of snow around him. A few broken bricks lay on the ground, a trickle of smoke leaking out of the chimney.

"Everyone okay?" he asked.

"Yeah, some smoke and ashes, I swept it up and the fire was out at the time. But no fire for Christmas now, the kids will be disappointed."

"It'll be okay," John said. "We'll survive."

CHRYSALIS

❦

It was a Christmas tradition that John and Laura would stay up late, drinking wine and talking, giving thanks for the year behind them. Laura would glance at the presents and John would wince. Every time she left the room, he poured his wine into hers, preparing for the night ahead.

At one o'clock he tucked her into bed and went out to the truck. It was cold outside, getting colder, the layers he wore giving him little protection. There was a slow snowfall gracing the crops, his headlights pushing out into the night. John was numb. Where was the storm, the epic snowfall, the crushing ice storm, the arctic temperature littering the countryside with the dead?

He pulled up to the trailer and Jamie stepped outside. On the river was a single barge filled with coal. A crane was extended out over it, teeth gleaming in the moonlight.

"Ready?" Jamie asked.

"Yeah."

Jamie manned the crane, back and forth, filling it up with coal and turning it to the side, a shower of black falling on the truck bed, the darkness filling with the impact of the coal. Over and over again Jamie filled the crane with coal and turned it to the truck bed, and released it. In no time the bed was overflowing.

"That's all she'll hold, John," Jamie said.

"Thanks, Jamie. You might want to take some home yourself."

"Why?"

"Storm coming."

At the house, he backed the truck up to the chute, glancing up at the sky, clear and dark, with stars dotting the canvas. He opened the heavy metal doors that lead into the basement and started shoveling the coal down into the chute—the coal sliding down and spilling onto the floor. Fat snowflakes started to fall, a spit of drizzle that quickly turned to ice, slicing at his face. He kept shoveling. The bed of the truck was an eternity stretching into the night—one slick blackness pushing out into another. He kept on. The snow fell harder, John struggling to see much of anything, guessing where the mouth of the chute was, flinging the coal into the gaping hole, feeding the hungry beast.

When he was done he didn't move the truck. He could hardly lift his arms. And his secret wouldn't last much longer, anyway. In the kitchen he sat under the glow of the dim bulb that was over the sink, sipping at a pint of bourbon that he had pulled out of the glove box, numb and yet sweating, nauseous and yet calm. It was done. Whatever would come, it was done.

He fell into a fitful slumber, his wife asleep beside him, the silence of the building snowfall, deafening.

The morning brought screams of joy, and soon after that, screams of panic and fear. The children climbed in bed, excited to open their presents, bouncing on the heavy comforter as Laura beamed at the children. John sat up, dark circles and puffy flesh under his red, squinting eyes.

"John, you look terrible, you okay?"

"We'll see," he said. He leaned over and kissed her. "Just know that I love you," he said.

Laura turned to the kids. "Should we go downstairs?"

"Mommy, look at all the snow. Everything is white," Missy said.

Laura got up and walked to the window.

"My God. John, come here."

John stood up and walked over to the window, the yard filled with snow, a good four feet up the trunk of an old oak tree. The snow showed no sign of stopping. The limbs were covered in ice, hanging low. John walked to the other window that faced into the back yard, and saw that only the cab of his truck was visible above the snow.

The kids turned and ran down the stairs. Laura turned to John and opened her mouth, and then closed it. When they got to the bottom of the stairs the kids were already at the presents, starting to rip them open. Coal dust and fingerprints were on the stockings, a small bulge at the bottom of each. They stopped at the bottom of the steps and watched the kids as their smiles turned to looks of dismay.

"John, what's going on," Laura asked.

The kids looked up, the boxes empty. Missy went to her stocking and dumped the lump of coal into her hand. John didn't remember putting those lumps of coal in the stockings. Some of last night was a blur. Outside the wind picked up. The loose bricks shifted in the fireplace, a dull thud scattering across the roof, and a blur of red fell past the window.

Missy began to cry.

"John, what did you do?" Laura's face was flush, and she walked to Missy, pulling the girl to her side. Jed kept ripping open boxes, his face filling with rage—any box, big or small—his name, Missy's name, he kept ripping them open.

Empty, all of them.

John sat on the couch and clicked on the television set, all of their voices filling the room, the paper tearing, Missy crying, Laura saying his name over and over again.

" . . . for the tri-county area. Temperatures are plummeting down into the negatives, currently at minus 20 and falling, wind chill of thirty below zero. We are expecting anywhere from six to ten feet of snow. That's right, I said ten feet."

"Shut up!" John yelled, turning to them, tears in his eyes. He turned back to the television set.

"Winds upward of fifty miles an hour. We have power outages across the state. So far over fifty thousand residents are without electricity. ComEd trucks are crippled as the snow is falling faster than the plows can clear them. Already we have reports of municipal vehicles skidding off the icy roads."

John looked up into the corner of the room where a large spider web was spreading. A ladybug was caught in the strands, no longer moving. The weatherman kept talking, but John could no longer hear him. The map, the charts, the arrows and numbers spread across the television screen, warnings and talk of death on the roads.

" . . . anywhere from six to ten days before . . . "

Outside there is a cracking sound, a heavy, deep ripping and the kids run to the window and look out. Icicles and branches fall to the ground, shattering like glass, half of the tree tearing off, one mighty branch falling to the ground, shaking the foundation, sending snow flying up into the air.

"John?" Laura says.

" . . . do not go outside for anything . . . "

"John?"

" . . . blankets, huddle together . . . "

Somewhere down the road a transformer blows sending sparks into the sky, the bang startling the kids who start to cry, burrowing deeper into Laura's side.

" . . . police and a state of emergency . . . "

The television set goes black and the Christmas tree lights wink off. Winds beat against the side of the house as a shadow passes over the windows. Outside the snow falls in an impermeable blanket, the roads and trees no longer visible.

The room is suddenly cold.

John gets up and goes to the kitchen, taking a glass out from the cabinet and turns on the water. There is a dull screeching sound as the whole house shakes, and nothing comes out of the tap.

"Pipes are frozen," John says to himself.

On the windowsill is a line of candles, and three flashlights sitting in a row. He grabs one of the flashlights and opens the basement door, staring down into the darkness. John walks down the stairs to where the coal spills across the concrete, grabbing a shovel that he has leaned against the wall. He pulls open one furnace door, then the other, and setting the flashlight on the ground so that is shoots up at the ceiling, he shovels in the coal. In no time the furnace is full. He walks around the basement, the band of light reflecting off the ductwork, turning screws and opening vents. Behind him on the stairs Laura stands with the children in front of her, each of them holding a lit candle, a dull yellow illuminating their emotionless faces. John lights a match and tosses it into the furnace, a dull whoomp filling up the room.

Turning back to his family at the top of the steps, John smiles, and wipes the grime off of his face.

LOVE LETTERS

IT STARTED WITH the paper, tearing it apart into little pieces, pressing it into tiny balls and popping the crumpled words into her mouth. Cassidy would chew and chew his love letters while staring out the window, the sun setting across the city—her apartment falling into darkness. She imagined that she could hear him speaking, his deep voice filling up the empty spaces that she created with her desperation and remorse. He compared her to a summer day, to a moonlit lake, to a drug addiction—one he needed to quit. She didn't believe he would disappear—Cassidy felt their love was eternal. Twirling her long, red hair in slender, pale fingers, she stared out at the city, wondering where he was.

She moved on to the ink. In an effort to embrace a historical sense of romance, she purchased an inkwell and a quill, inserting the sharp tip into the shimmering black liquid, running the tip across the page. It didn't turn out well. When she hesitated, and that was often, she would place the tip of the quill on her tongue and tap it, tap it, trying to put in words her feelings for him, the man who spent many a night caressing her ivory skin while whispering in her ear. Soon enough her stomach rolled and flipped, tightening into knots of anguish, vomiting a great void into the toilet, her lips and teeth stained with death.

She crafted her own perfume, a mortar and pestle sitting on her kitchen counter, grinding up bits of sandalwood, pounding out waxy pieces of ambergris, slicing her finger over the stone bowl, crying into it, squeezing out blood orange, adding a few drops of honey. She poured this lumpy mixture through screen after another, the weave getting smaller, until the essence was but a spoonful in a bowl. She rubbed it in her fingers, behind her ears, her kneecaps, and ran it across the envelope seal, dropping her letter in the mail. To no avail—he didn't notice.

When his silence filled her mailbox, a slender rectangle of metal and failure, she took up her needle and thread, to immortalize his final words, the last letter he sent to her, signing off with the words that haunted her now, caused her to flinch—love always the lie that he kept telling. She took a deep breath and ran the needle under her skin, a muffled gasp, her heart quickening, his love still finding a way to her heart. She pulled the thread through, up and down, the script filling her left forearm, a reminder of the things men say, a warning to the next fool that would certainly share her bed, a love letter to herself.

Vision Quest

THE FROZEN PACK of peas that I hold to my forehead can't block out the noise of broken glass and twisted metal. Last night was another failed opportunity, one of many in a long line of failed evenings spent racing battered cars around the city, aiming for brick walls and concrete dividers. I was trying to undo the mental anguish that had come home to rest on my shoulders with a crippling weight. The others don't understand me, they want what I have, hoping that their slippery catch will yield fewer teeth than mine, that their visions aren't hauntings—shadows of my past.

The dark helps. The shades are drawn down behind thick curtains, the recliner leaned way back, the bag on my head, the television set muted, flashes of color sending icy spikes through my temples, so I close my eyes and take a breath. When the weight of my long dead cat settles into my lap, hot tears push out of my eyes, and I ask him to go away. But he won't. This is where he always rested, where he came to sit and purr, the vibrations thrumming my legs, so I have no choice but to pet the long-haired beast, the swollen tumor in his throat distended, as his outline shimmers in the dimly lit living room. The house is empty now, too large for my newly solitary life, but it's the only thing I have left of them, and I'm unwilling to let it all go.

I can't explain it, nobody can. The medical doctors just refer me to psychiatrists and those shrinks only prescribe pills that dull the edges, nodding their heads and using words like "closure" and "release."

I hear cars outside on the street, the world slipping by, and I wonder how I got here. Accident, what does that word mean—random, unintentional? Accidental. Accidents. We all have them. I'm having them all the time now.

An innocent phone call led to a deafening silence, to a morgue in a concrete bunker that I never knew existed. Every detail made my hands shake, my head throb, the officer with his hand on my shoulder, his fingers gripping into my dead muscle, the black bags pulled back one by one, each one worse than the previous devastating knowledge.

My wife was first, asleep on the cold metal, the gash across her head the only obvious sign of the violence that started my undoing.

"You okay?" the man asked. He kept asking it over and over.

The twins were next, still in grade school when the minivan skidded off the icy road, barely in second grade.

My son, a lump on the side of his head, a seam running up the front of his chest, his tiny ribcage, and I thought of birds, wanting to get out, trying to push against the bars, and I turned and vomited into a plastic trash can that the man standing next to me held out. A cop, the morgue guy, I can't remember who he really was. I try not to think about it.

VISION QUEST

My daughter, I only had to look at her hand, the pink fingernails, with Hello Kitty appliqués looking up at me, forlorn.

"Don't pull it back. Please," I asked. But he did anyway. And everything went dark.

That was the first accident, the one that started it all. Left to my own devices I started to drink, whatever was in the house, everything, all of it, until the next thing I knew I came to flying down the highway at eighty miles an hour.

That's never a good thing.

$\sim$

It took me awhile to start calling people. I just couldn't muster the strength. It wasn't real to me—I didn't want to own it. But eventually I started calling family—mothers and grandmothers, brothers and sisters, all of it painful until it stopped being anything but a headache, a tension in my gut, snakes uncoiling inside me. They started showing up and I went through the motions, the crying and the hugging, and eventually they faded away, back to their cities and lives, afraid to catch what I had brewing inside me. I understood. I welcomed their departures. The insurance check came in and I quit my job, not that I had been going, and decided to drink myself to death. It seemed like the right thing to do.

It was an easy choice, barreling down the highway, flashers in the rear view mirror, and little left that mattered. All I had to do was pull the wheel hard to the left, and the moment the thought entered my head, I did it. Maybe it was an accident, a twitch.

The tires squealed, and the car flipped over, blackness wrapping around me, a smile pushing across my face, dots of white light—my head making contact with something. I wanted this, wished it to be over, the sickening momentary panic of my head being crushed, the sense that this was more pain and more serious than anything I'd ever experienced. That revelation flashed across my mind, and then everything winked out.

A hospital, several tickets, uniforms in blue, uniforms in white. I couldn't do this right either, the seatbelt saving my life, a life I had no interest in saving. A new word was bandied about the room, as I drifted in and out, pain radiating out of my misshapen skull, broken fingers, broken legs, broken ribs. The word of the day was "lucky" and it made me laugh until blood sprayed out of my mouth, a coughing fit, and then they pushed me back under with meds and hands on my cold flesh, and the pale outline of my daughter standing next to the bed, shaking her head slowly back and forth, disappointed in my reckless behavior.

❧

Amy and Robb were friends, people I used to work with. Amy was a slightly overweight, loud-mouthed blonde who made me laugh. She was always placing her hand on my forearm, always touching me. I didn't mind it so much now. Robb wore glasses and a black Kangol hat, skinny and pale, a moustache and goatee giving him the odd appearance of a foreign filmmaker, or perhaps an unemployed mime. They came to visit me in the hospital, and followed up with random drop-ins at the house, forgiving in their judgment, bringing chicken wings and beer, absorbing my pain, listening with tight lips and barely nodding heads as I told them about my shadow daughter, and the recent reappearance of my cat.

"It's stress," Amy offered. "You're just dealing with it all, processing. I'm sure it's nothing."

Robb nodded, sipping at his beer. "Yeah, stress. I'm sure that's all it is."

I didn't tell them about the day before when I walked past my daughter's room and saw her and my son playing on the floor, a bucket of Lego pieces scattered across the carpet, a brick wall built up in an array of colors, repeatedly running a tiny Lego car into the solid structure they'd built, over and over again. They looked up at me, and moved their lips and I stumbled over my own feet, moving past them without looking back, unable to mouth the words "I love you" in return.

In time I would tell Amy and Robb about that moment. I would tell them about my wife appearing in my bed, her arms wrapping around me, pressing her cold flesh up against my bare backside, her hand reaching around to rub my chest, nibbling at my neck, unable to stop her. I would tell them about all of this, about my dead wife turning me on, her hands wrapped around my cock, stroking me as her breasts pressed against my back, my eyes squeezed shut, pretending it was all a dream. When I washed the sheets later that day, I sobbed and bent over the washing machine, afraid to go back to bed.

I told them all of this because I couldn't keep it to myself.

"I've had worse wet dreams," Robb mused. "Don't

get me started. Clowns, old grade school teachers, a cousin I barely know, fairies farting sparks of glitter when they came."

Over time, they started to believe me. They muttered things about long lost relatives, ex-boyfriends that overdosed, bored with their lives, their office jobs and life in the suburbs. I laughed about my head injury, laughed about my visions. And as the nights expanded and the conversations continued, they would place their hands on my forehead, the bruise and the lump fading, making mental notes about the exact location.

When I told them about my son, his worried look, the note he left me scrawled in the foggy mirror of the bathroom one morning, the numbers 8 22 32 44 64 pushed together in his tiny fingered script, they swallowed their beer and leaned back onto the couch. They were always here now—this was better than watching TV, better than hanging out at some seedy bar. I was spending money on food and drink, plowing through it, buying a new car, and my ghost of a son was worried about the money. I spent some cash on a Little Lotto ticket, and collected $4,235.26 the following day. It wasn't much, but as he leaned over my head, pushing my hair out of the way, in the same way that I used to tuck him in, he told me that I didn't want any attention. Small steps, he whispered, pressing his damp lips onto my forehead, and I fell asleep shaking and cold.

〜

The first thing we did was cut all of the seatbelts out of

my new car. It pained me to do this to a brand new Mustang, but it made sense—no chickens in this ride. I was trying to get out, and they were trying to get in. I'd look in the rearview mirror at Amy and Robb, giddy as two kids heading off for ice cream, and shake my head.

"My brother," Amy said, one night on the couch, one of many lost nights that we spent talking about this new endeavor. "He died in high school. Ironically, in a car accident, drunk as a skunk," she said. "I want to see him again."

"My first wife killed herself," Robb said, swallowing another beer, head bowed. "I need to talk to her, I have questions. I need to say I'm sorry," he mumbled.

I understood. It wasn't the money—I shared the numbers that my flickering son whispered in my ear, we cashed in our tickets for a couple grand here or there, every once in awhile a bigger score, ten grand or more. We couldn't keep winning, he told me that, we had to drive to Indiana, or up to Wisconsin, spread it around, and take turns buying the tickets. It wasn't about the money. We had nobody to share our spoils with anyway. We were three loners connected by the thrill of doing something that nobody else could do.

I looked into the back seat as I accelerated up the entrance ramp onto the highway.

"You're just going to end up dead," I yelled.

They held hands and smiled. On the seat next to me my wife sat in shadow, her face away from me, staring out the window into the night. Silver tears ran dirty paths down her cheeks, a weary smile crooked across her face. She didn't want me to join them on the other side. And yet, she did. The rules. Who knew what they were? I only knew that the pale imitation of life that I held onto with my weak grip—it didn't mean anything to me anymore. On either side of Amy and Robb, the twins sat somber, frightened by it all, eyes on me, and yet, unable to really look at me, wanting me to hold them again, to feel my warmth, but afraid to ask me to do this, the violence a terrifying unknown.

We were sober tonight, facing this obstacle head on. I punched the gas on the new Mustang, the pang in my stomach the only bit of life left in me. I wanted her to say no, my wife, but she didn't say anything. I wanted the kids to say we'll wait for you—we'll be here whenever you get here, twenty years down the road. But they didn't say those words.

I pushed us out into the night, my wife's cold hand resting on my thigh, and I pulled the steering wheel to the left, looking up into the rearview mirror, Robb's mouth open, as if poised to say something, his eyebrows arched mid-question. Amy's eyes were glassy and distant, far away, knowing that one way or another she'd see her brother soon. And my daughter, her head down, unable to face me, my son with his hands in his lap, they looked up in unison, a slow grin spreading across their distorted features, a secret held in their mouths—and the car flipped us over and into the great beyond.

SURRENDER

IN THE PROCESS of losing my mind, the rest of the world has fallen away. A cloud hangs over the monotone house, the grass growing longer, the litter outside caught in the wild blades of fading green, as the shadows inside play games with me. I used to resist them, tried to shine a light into the corners of the living room, the drapes—the long hallways that never seemed to end. I used to scream at them, crying as I fell to my knees, begging to be left alone. When I walk by the bedroom now, the door closed, a cold wave pushing out from under the gaps, nipping at my ankles, I moan quietly under my breath as a shadow flickers at the door frame. I do not open it, not now.

I grew up around this house, with its curving banister, the old grandfather clock that sat in the foyer, the secret passageways between bedrooms hundreds of years old. I loved to spend time here, to open the glass candy dish and see what Grandma had put out that day, to hide in the bedroom closets and wait for my brother to find me. Now, I only see death.

When my grandmother passed away I was sad, of course, the memories of so many holidays spent here, Christmas trees crowded by presents, the whole family gathered around the Thanksgiving table. That all changed. It changed so fast that I never saw it coming. I couldn't fathom what lurked in the darkness, what waited for me to come home.

For a long time now I've stared at the ceiling, sleeping on the antique couch, covered in dust, afraid to go upstairs, but afraid to leave it as well. I know how it summons—I know how it pulls the light to it and snuffs it out. So I stay and ask myself what I did to bring this spirit to me, what actions and crimes I committed to lure the demon out. In the dark, no amount of blankets are able to stop my shivering, I hear it upstairs, heavy footsteps, the weight of lead boots, the mass of flesh a horrible density, the shadows always fading to cold air. I remember the abortion, the way my girlfriend cried—this selfish act that we hid from the world, drowned in our sorrows and a river of amber liquid. I remember the anxiety of a thump in the road, the radio blaring, the shape left behind as I drove on, turned away, vomiting in the bushes later, pretending that nothing had happened. I remember the heroin, the needles and the glossy cold skin she wore, the way we would pour into each other, our mouths hot for slick tongues, our fingers eager to grab, to clench, to slide inside. She deserved better—I know that now. The only sound left from that night, from the dense woods, from the dull panic that washed over me is the sound of the shovel blade piercing the earth, over and over again.

Nobody thought anything of the gray cat, the Maine Coon we called Quixotic, passing away in the middle of the night. He was fifteen years old, moving slow already, doomed to die in this house—we all knew that. And yet, as I fell asleep that night, his cries came

SURRENDER

to me from the basement, wrapped in an urgency that made me queasy, that made me hesitate, pull back the covers and sit up on the edge of the bed. I heard him make his way up the stairs, and heard him slump to the floor in the guest room, and assumed he was fine, when he finally went quiet.

Guest room. Yes, that's accurate. Our guest.

We buried him in the back yard, the acre of old oaks a canopy stretching over our heads, the brick fireplace where we would barbeque and gather, the chipped fountain of a forlorn boy spouting water into its cracked base. I have a hard time saying their names now, my son, my wife—they have turned to smoke and drifted away. My son, Robert, he took the sticks, wound round with yarn, the simple placard reading "Quicky," as we called the cat, and pushed into the earth with a sigh. That night as we fell asleep, my sadness a heavy weight on my chest, the place the cat used to sit and purr, a series of doors slammed shut, a groaning from the pipes in the basement, and we clung to each other, my Linda disappearing in my arms, tears and darkness and heavy sighs luring us to sleep. We were not afraid, not yet. We were sad, and tired, and ready to move on. Our guest was not.

I didn't know much about electricity, so my brother William helped me with the ceiling fan. It seemed a simple task. The guest room was always hot, except when it was cold, needing a false breeze to keep the stillness from growing. The circuit breakers, they were flipped. The light from the windows was barely enough, clouds drifting over the yard, but we did not hesitate. A ladder, the wires, screws and a drill, it was nothing to us, an easy job, a task to be done. There

-41-

were cold beers and a back porch waiting for us later, the inevitability of it unquestioned. I slapped him on the back, and we hoisted the fan. And then he grabbed the wires.

There were no lights on in the room, and yet I stared at him as his body shook, as his eyes bulged and a darkness swept across the room, the ladder shaking, no voice in my chest, no words in my mouth, the smell of charred flesh, the urine pooling beneath the ladder, his body falling to the ground, the fan crashing down on us, as I muttered his name over and over, smoke drifting as tendrils to the ceiling where it gathered. The room now held an anxious weight.

There never would be a fan in that room, the broken blades and glass carted out to the garbage cans in the quiet of the next day, the wires sticking out of the hole, always pointing, always reaching out for more. And in the corners of the room, the shadows grew, the air thick with the stench of burnt flesh.

The house had changed for us now, and we stayed away from the guest room, closing the door, which always reopened, stayed on the north side of the house, leaving that hallway alone. And yet, we went on. It was still weeks before I'd start killing myself, there was still an air of hope.

Still in a fog, we snapped at each other, my wife and I, over every small thing, over every task not done a certain way. We spit our angry words at each other over garbage cans and their liners, over bills that had not been paid, over loose handrails and crooked pictures and dinners that we brought home in greasy paper bags. Maybe we could have run then, maybe it was still forming, still weak. I don't know.

SURRENDER

The sounds that came to us as we fought in the kitchen, they did not make any sense, they had no context in our memories. We stomped and pointed, we clenched our fists and spewed obscenities, faces flushed, as the house around us creaked and moaned, the doors opening and closing, the boy running from room to room, a game he was playing, certainly, a laugh on his lips as he amused himself, certainly not terrified, not running from something, not trying to escape, just playing as boys are known to do. My fist banged on the table, a tall thin water glass breaking in the kitchen sink as Linda turned her back to me, cursing into the hot water that flowed over the dirty dishes. Our heads turned with a snap at the pounding, the heavy thuds as they repeated down the curving staircase, over and over until we were met with the eventual silence of the boy hitting the hardwood floor. No words, just a gasp, eyes widening, and we ran out of the room, muttering to our absent God, and found him bent and broken, lying still on the floor.

There was not much left after that, I think. There was no color, or light, only darkness. People came and left, the house was full and then empty, things were done, paperwork, I imagine, nothing that stays with me, nothing that matters. I often found myself wandering the hallways, cold and yet sweating, standing in the guest room, arms at my side, a cloak of black wrapping around me, as I cursed the shadows, begged it to take me. I was done. A dirty teddy bear sat in the corner, a long line of Matchbox cars leading from it to the edge of my shoes, and my head filled with swarming bees, my eyes rolled up into the back of my head, and I collapsed.

Linda is at our bedside, her hands on my wrist, her voice a whisper, and she's telling me something, that we have to leave, that she's leaving, that it's all gone now, nothing left—I can't decipher what she's saying. I cannot move. She tells me it is too much and I can barely nod. Go, I tell her, there's nothing here for you. I have nothing left to offer. Run. I close my eyes and she is gone.

I open them and there is a pounding at the front door, lights flashing and I cannot speak to the men in uniform, as they pour past me into the house, as the smell of something burning fills the hallway and my mouth. They are in the kitchen shouting and there is a wave of smoke, the sound of water, the cursing and grunting of men. They ask for my wife, they mention the boy, my brother—they have been here before. I am mute. There is water on the floor, a puddle in which I stand, and as I look above my head there is an irregular shape on the ceiling above, the guest bathroom, the drip, drip, dripping filling the air with a metronome, a repetition that wants to add up to something.

There is more noise upstairs, men yelling and I still cannot move. I am pushed out of the way, as a stretcher flies past me, the man in charge, his hand on my arm, yelling at me from underwater, pushing me into a chair, a flashlight in my eyes, and there are doctors, paramedics, policemen, firemen, a flurry of action, and I am slipping into a comatose skin, my flesh gone alabaster, my heart freezing into stone. The last thing I remember is the slashes of red on the white, white sheet—and she is gone from me forever.

I told her to run. He didn't let her get away.

Time has abandoned me; I am no longer alive—I

SURRENDER

am no longer human. I get in the car and drive and drive, out onto the highway into the darkness, the world around me lacking clarity, and I find myself back in the driveway, the engine running—the car door open wide. I pick up the telephone and call anybody who will answer, beg them to come get me, to get me away from this unholy presence, and then I wait downstairs for the doorbell to ring, but they never show up.

There is a vague memory of a hammer and nails, of boards. There is the smell of gasoline leaking from under the door and the matches in my hand will not strike. There is a pinching at my wrists and a feeling of great release and I awake in my bed, naked, claw marks up and down my skin, bite marks on my shoulders and the torn flesh on my arms is stitched together with long pieces of dark, sinewy hair.

When there is nothing left, when I have finally surrendered, no longer seeking absolution, no longer praying to any God, anywhere, no longer ignoring the price I now must pay, not at my hands, but at his, I take the hammer and I claw at the wood, I pull away the barrier to the closed off room, this abyss, this dark sanctuary, and I place my hands on the cold metal knob—I turn it slowly and breath frost into the air, I give myself over to the darkness inside, and finally, he swallows me whole.

THE WASTELANDS

DARKNESS POURS ACROSS empty desert. The behemoth trudges toward the fire pit with his massive wooden bowl, spilling the shriveled raisins, dreams deferred, into the gaping maw that cleaved the earth. I could fire my worn rifle at his thick hide, but it wouldn't do any good. He lumbers back to the city and out of my sight, the steel collar around his neck dotted with spikes and a single yellow square of flashing light. They track him now. He tends to wander.

My lair is carved out of a mountain. The only way to traverse the flat stone is a long slender rope with knots tied every couple of feet. I hide out here, waiting for something to change, for someone to tell me that things will get better. I'm doubtful. In the distance I see the tiny outline of the creature as he heads back to the glass and metal that has enslaved so many—but not me.

When the rules fell and anarchy took over the country, I tried to blend in, to become one of the unthinking—to keep my family in line. When they came to take the children for the mines, and my wife for the hospital, a breeder now, it seemed, I went at them with clenched teeth and was beaten into submission. The decision unfurled in the blink of an eye, the crack of a rifle butt against my skull. If I had my way, there would be no survivors. Wrestling the weapon from the man in black canvas, his visor shut, a eunuch, I opened fire on the swarm of dead mannequins that poured into our apartment. I did not discriminate. When the children fell to the side, stepped on, stabbed, limbs snapping, my wife's screams piercing the thud of boot steps, I kept on pulling the trigger.

In the end, I stood over my broken boy and placed the muzzle against his tear-streaked face, looked away and ended his life. My girl was already silent—the weeping, I realized, was coming from me. My wife looked up at me, her long hair matted in crimson, her lips swollen and torn, a sneer rippling across her bruised and shattered face.

"Do it," she said. "Wipe it clean."

I knelt down and held her face in my hands as she sobbed quicksilver, choking on her own blood.

"Do something that matters," she said.

I kissed her forehead and stood up, pushing the rifle toward her. She opened her mouth and fellated the barrel, one last spark in her eyes, and the sharp crack filled the room with a hollow finality.

A flutter of black and I'm standing on the edge of the cave, staring down at the endless void, the bats stitching the night sky with their angry chirps and leathery wings. With a heavy sigh I retreat into the back, hungry again, yet sick to my stomach, wanting to vomit it all away, but knowing such weakness will get me nowhere. Instead, I think of the beast, the great destroyer and his endless treks from the city to my front door.

THE WASTELANDS

"Do something that matters," her voice echoes into the darkness, and I fall into a fitful sleep. A sleep where my dreams are choked by the succubus and her wanting mouth, her promises to help me most certainly lies, but lies that may be my only hope. Long hair that reeks of the dead brushes over my face, and she is on me.

                              ∽

"Give it to me," she says.

Oil swims atop water and she covers me entirely. I am held down, and yet, lifted up. Her tongue is a writhing snake that fills my mouth. Her heavy breasts with hard nipple tips rest on my scratched and bleeding chest, her long fingernails pressing into my shoulders, her glossy heat enveloping my aching desire. I can't resist her, though I'd like to—she's too strong. So I pull her to me, my hands running up her narrow waist, and back down to clench her slick ass beneath my fingers, pulling her to me, pushing her down, impaling her on my cock. She moans and speaks the language of the dead, muttering prayers and curses, flies buzzing around my head, landing on my sticky face, rocks and twigs digging into my back, each thrust another cut and tear, another pinprick of pain. Her muscles tighten as she drains me dry, pulling every last drop of my life out into her barren womb, in search of a way to continue her malformed lineage, to push it forward and out into the wastelands.

And then it's cold. She is gone. And I am left to wither in the dirt, clinging to her promises, her barter. A stench of rotten milk and rancid grease fills the room. In my diseased state, I flicker and pass out.

I throw the rope down and descend into the night. The moon is high and full, but it offers little comfort. I must get rid of her stench, so I limp to a spring that sputters nearby and wash away her dirty work, rubbing my stinging flesh with jasmine flowers and orange rinds. The water is warm, and stinks of sulfur, but it's the best I can do.

I sit in the warm water, and wait for her offerings to materialize. Soon, a small brown rabbit bounds up to me, and stops, its red eyes glowing in the dark. It twitches a pink nose and eases forward, uncertain and shaking, but it keeps moving nonetheless. When it lays its trembling head in my lap, I pass my gnarled hands over the soft fur, petting the beast, remembering a time when domesticated animals would offer up waves of unconditional love. And then I snap its neck. I will eat today.

In the early grey hours of morning, the smell of cooking rabbit meat makes my stomach roll. The fire spits and cracks, my mouth wet and eager. I wait for her other gift to arrive, taking the sticks off of the flame, chewing on the moist haunches of the first bit of life I've seen up close in months. Shame. I gnaw the meat down to the bone, trying hard not to picture it gazing up at me, the surrender that filled its simple eyes.

When the raven lands next to me, I am not

surprised. It pecks at the bones, glassy orbs darting here and there, stepping from one black shriveled claw to the other. It bobs its head and inches closer to me, unhappy with my meager offerings. When it is close enough, I shoot my right arm out and grab it around the neck, its beak bending back, picking at my hand, my arm, tearing up strips of flesh. I reach beside me for a battered old screwdriver, the handle worn smooth by my sweat. I jab it into the belly of the squirming black bird and it stops moving. A metal door flips open from beneath its ruffled feathers, batteries spilling to the dirt floor, with an assortment of springs and sprockets.

I prop the quiet machine in my lap and go to work. It will take some time, but she has whispered into my ears on many a night, so the task is not impossible. Screws are turned, and wires re-routed, a lever pulled, a switch flipped, and when I push the metal opening shut with a barely audible click, I whisper my name into the raven's microphone, and command it to obey my every wish. We spend several hours executing orders and testing out the newly wired upgrade, and the raven is eager to do what I ask. When I notice the sun withering in the sky, I place the bird on my shoulder, pick up my rifle, and head down the rope to the dirt floor below. He'll be here soon.

I don't know what he is, exactly—some combination of gigantism and steroids, no doubt. But he is human, I know that much. Or I've been told. So I sit on an outcropping of half-buried boulders at the edge of the burning pit and wait for the beast to arrive.

It doesn't take long.

The ground vibrates under his heavy feet, and I can

soon enough see him approaching, the heavy carved bowl filling his arms, the whisper of a thousand voices babbling and screaming, the cries of the living to be buried among the dead. I've held on to my dreams, out here in the desert, but many are not as fortunate as me. False gods and empty rhetoric fill the streets, the airwaves, the masses stumbling forward with little hope remaining. I can't save them all. But I can resurrect my own, I think. That is all that I ask.

When the beast is within my line of sight I stand up and turn my head to the bird. He takes off in a straight line for the lumbering golem, circling his head, cawing and flapping its wings, landing on his shoulder. He turns his swollen head to the tiny bird and eyes it with delight. He takes two steps toward the crack in the earth and dumps the shriveled black bowl of insanity into the fires and casts the ton of wood aside like a boy skipping rocks.

"Birdie," he says, holding out his arm, and the raven hops out and alights on his extended index finger. A misshapen grin destroys his face—teeth like tombstones, dented and gray.

"Hey, buddy," I yell.

The giant looks down, noticing me for the first time. A scowl dims his face and I can see where this is headed. The hand without the bird resting on it turns into a tight fist.

"It's okay," I say. "He's yours. It's a present from me to you."

"Present?" he asks.

His fist unclenches and he looks at the bird.

"Long time," he says. "Long time from presents."

He turns back to me, eyes squinting.

"You? You want?" he asks.

"Just a ride," I say. "Back to the city. Beyond the gates."

"Gates?"

"Inside," I say.

"Inside," he echoes.

His massive head nods up and down. He shrugs his shoulders.

Bending over he says, "Get on."

I hop up onto his shoulders and he rises back up, my stomach clenching.

"Mine?" he asks. "Forever?"

"Forever."

He moves forward, the raven flying out and back, landing on his finger. Out and back, out and back, like a dog fetching an imaginary stick—and the mountain of a man chuckles to himself.

I can hear the voice of my wife, her lips on my ear, my neck. She is nuzzling me, her hand on my back, and at my side I feel small fingers, grasping at my hand, taking my fingers in theirs.

～

Truth and lies, they are the same. Police state, chaos, or only the inevitable—the gap has been growing, the separation expanding, the outside influence of foreign nations penetrating, until nothing remains of what was once a flourishing land of opportunity.

The narrow black towers that stand quiet in the desert crackle to life when the beast approaches the gate.

"Where's your bowl?" a speaker booms.

The spotlights track back and forth on the ground at his feet. The raven rests in his tangled hair, as I hide on the other side of his head.

"Where's your bowl, you invalid," the voice shouts. He bows his head slightly and responds to the guard.

"Lost it."

A muttering seeps over the airwaves.

"He lost another one. Idiot."

The gates buzz and he lumbers through the opening, and into the city, grumbling to himself. He holds out his hand and the raven obliges, flying out and back, landing on his finger. He grins and bends over, and I hop off of his shoulders, scamper into the darkness and disappear.

I hold the rifle to the doctor's throat and hand him the handful of teeth, hair and dried bits of flesh that I've kept in a canvas bag, tied to my waist, for these many lonely years. Surrounding us are tables of pale flesh, some covered with cloth, others connected to tubes, the sharp bite of chemicals, embalming fluids and formaldehyde.

It was a mistake, I realize. Whatever horrors await us, we will face them together—I was wrong.

"How long?" I ask him.

"Nine months, maybe a little less."

"And they'll be okay, they'll be normal?"

"Yes," he says, "We've come a long way from Dolly. This ain't my first rodeo."

I can only remember them the way they were, and that's the way they will return to me. Not younger, not lying in their own blood, but the way they were before that—happy.

⌒

When the bombing starts, I think I've been discovered, that somehow the doctor has figured out where I am. But they miss me. They only succeed in widening the gap, the great bowels filled with fire widening to spread the heat and destruction. When he stops coming, the simple giant who has become my only friend, I fear the worst. And on those nights when she comes for me, the harpy with her dirty talons, her teeth nipping at my greasy flesh, I can hardly push her away.

What does it matter now, I wonder?

But he shows himself eventually, the only excuse, the only reason for his absence a shiny new bowl with which to carry the dead dreams of the masses. The raven flits about his head like a gnat in the shimmering heat, landing on the lip of the bowl, cawing and bobbing his head.

This time, however, the bowl is silent. He bends down onto one knee and places the polished wood in the dirt, setting it gently on the ground, tipping it over with the grace and patience of a saint. I stand before the turning wood, staring into the darkness, my throat clenched shut.

When my family runs to me and wraps their arms around my tattered frame, I hold them to me. The only words that can escape my lips are the same pleas for mercy and understanding that I will offer to the bent gods for the rest of my life.

"Please forgive me."

MISTY

I DIDN'T ASK where she went at night. Although, in hindsight, I suppose that I should have. It had been hard enough to lure her home, long black hair, bruised lips, curves that made my head spin, and eyes that tracked me like a cat. Not a housecat, for sure, but something long and slinky, always on the prowl, hiding in the shadows where the green slits sparkled and danced. Misty. That's what she told me anyway, and I went with it. Wasn't going to ask her for any ID. I had her digits, and she answered now and then, but it wasn't my place to tell her anything. I took what I could get.

"Bobby, you're all out of toilet paper," she screamed from the bathroom.

"Under the sink, baby, should be a couple rolls left."

"Thanks, hon," she said, sticking her head out of the steamy doorway, nothing but a fluffy white towel between her slick, warm flesh and my own scattered heartbeat. The room filled with the sweet scent of currant, the candle burning on the nightstand, the only thing she ever left behind.

It wasn't much of an apartment, but I wasn't much of a man. A long series of tragedies and failures trailed me like oily exhaust. I'd given up my hopes and dreams a long time ago. Scars and tattoos dotted my flesh, a series of jobs keeping me in the dark—bouncer and doorman, shipping and delivery—anything that required a bit of muscle and little thought. It was one bedroom that opened into a living room where a beat up green couch sat facing a scarred and worn out table, the flat screen the only bit of technology in the place. A drafty kitchen with dark tile held an ancient stove and refrigerator that were utilitarian at best. Salvation Army, Good Will, these were the places I looked for jeans and sweatshirts, thick wool sweaters and faded leather jackets—it didn't matter much to me. I saved whatever cash I had for the bottle.

Propped up on my elbows, I watched her get dressed. The black lace panties and push up bra were what I expected, her pale skin like alabaster, her eyes always darting to me, her tongue licking lips that I ached to bite. But I couldn't show her any weakness. She didn't respond well to need. It was the nights she wore the plain white cotton panties, the soft T-shirt with no bra on at all, the hints at a previous life, something domestic and safe, those were the moments when I thought I stood a chance of keeping her.

"I won't be back tonight, Bobby, got things to do," she said.

I nodded, still under the covers, naked, worn out from bourbon, pool and the aerobics her flesh required. I wanted her to go, but I wanted her to stay.

"Okay, Misty. Do what you gotta do," I said, a treble of whine under the detachment that got me a set of squinting eyes. "No worries, babe. I understand."

She exhaled and nodded, pulling on a pair of black

combat boots, standing up as she buttoned her skintight jeans, already out the door. I thought maybe she stripped; that wouldn't be out of the question. She didn't seem like a dealer, but you never know—a handful of pills, some powders and liquids, it wouldn't be hard for her to slip in and out of whatever clubs or bars she haunted. She was pretty enough to get away with murder, but rough enough around the edges to keep the predators at a distance.

She walked over to the bed and leaned down, her hands on my chest, her tongue sliding into my mouth. She turned to go without saying a word.

"Be good," I said.

"Why start now?" she laughed, closing the door behind her with a click.

It didn't bother me to see her sucking dick in a back alley. The guy looked loaded, and the pile of green he shoved in her pocket was probably her rent for the month. When he went inside, she spit on the ground and pulled a pint out of her pocket, swigging down a few gulps of amber, shoving her boot into a trashcan, the glass shattering on the brick wall. It was a reaction I could understand—respect even. The only way I'd want to see her act.

It didn't bother me to see her on stage, writhing around, pushing her hips into the air, shoving her crotch into the faces of bearded strangers, working the stage lights, her body electric, arousing me against all rhyme and reason. She wasn't my girl, that's for sure, and the scattered bills that covered the ground, she didn't even stop to pick them up. The frat boys and fading suburban fathers, they crowded around the center stage, AC/DC blasting, the flashing lights making my heart shudder, as she pinched her nipples with an angry scowl, running her black tipped fingers between her legs—really putting on a show. The troll that scampered around after she left, he picked up the bills into a nice stack and was off behind the curtain and into the darkness before her scent could even fade.

It was the other place she went. The drive north out of the city and toward the cornfields, the metal and glass fading into oblivion as the concrete stretched out into the night. I told myself to go back, to turn around, to keep what we had—our little secret—keep it going, don't ask for more than what you have. When she pulled off the highway and stopped at a grocery store, I started to get sick to my stomach, the thin plastic bags full of Kraft Macaroni and Cheese, a jug of orange juice, and a gallon of milk. I could see the transformation, the way her eyes softened as she flipped the radio dial, her head bobbing along to pop music, hair pulled back into a ponytail, turning into a subdivision of blue siding and white siding and yellow siding, one after another after another.

When she turned into the garage, there was movement behind the curtains, lights blocked by shadows, and then full again, a dull thud of a car door closing, while another opened, the screams and laughter drifting to my open window as I idled in the street by her mailbox, my left eye twitching, stomach contorted into knots.

"Mommy, mommy, she's home. Mommy's home."

THE HANDYMAN

DATALOG
2023:08.07

A.M.

My first stop is a housewife on the north shore. She doesn't ask me about the arm, and I'm pleasantly surprised. Most do. I like to mix it up. Sometimes it's a factory mishap, my arm torn off in a conveyor belt, the concrete slippery with oil and blood. Other times it's something more rural, a thresher that ripped it from the socket, the cornfield splashed with arcs of pumping liquid. Truth is I lost it to a needle, the golden sap my only life, my addiction, shooting up until the sores and pus disintegrated my arm at the elbow. They cut it off with lasers while I watched, the stench making my stomach buckle, and at the same time, hunger for a charred filet. The job is the usual digit work. I open a few jars and crimp a few pipes. I lift a piano, an armoire, the back end of her minivan—her two boys running around to rotate the tires, sweaty and laughing at the idiot lying there, his arm a piston powered jack.

P.M.

These are always the tricky ones, the ones at night. It's never anything that they want done in the light of the day. At the apartment on the edge of the city I find an empty room with a single bulb lit and barely swinging, suspended over a naked man tied to a metal chair. His eyes bulge when I enter the room and he shakes his head from side to side, the gag in his mouth restricting his words. I know better than to let him talk. They're never innocent.

I see a camera mounted in the upper right hand corner of this roach-infested slum, a sheet of plastic covering the floor. Nice touches, this one. She said her name was Amber, and the Voicescan told me she was speaking the truth—at least, the truth as far as she knew it. I'd come to trust the applications and instruments that had been built into my right arm. I carried a suitcase around with me, everything from screwdrivers and vice grips to handguns and blades. It took incoming data, via voice and email, complete with a slot for swiping, paying off the bill, and a data reader for the myriad of barcodes. Her payment had already cleared— an admission of anger and impatience. They never had the stomach, the ladies that hired me. It didn't matter much to me. This was what I did now. Days filled with construction, chores and general housework. Nights filled with the wet work. I opened the suitcase and pulled out a long, thin blade. Detaching the hand, I screwed the knife on and turned to the man.

"You know what you did. I'm not here to bargain."

His head shakes back and forth, and I exhale. Urine runs down the side of his leg as I nod at the camera and move in for the first cut. He's crying soon, muttering apologies as his nipples hit the floor, followed by the digits on his right hand, then the left. He's screaming soon after that, bucking in the chair, and to be honest, he's getting on my nerves. I turn to the camera again and nod my head, then run the blade across his throat. By the time I'm done attaching the saw blade the blinking light on the camera is dead. The limbs are severed and rolled in plastic. I attach the rib-spreader and dig into the ribcage, rummaging around for the heart. I vomit over the pile of appendages, the butterflied chest and the head that stares back at me, eyes open wide with shock.

DATALOG
2023:08.08

A.M.

She won't even get out of bed. And I know what she wants. Her skin is pale, and her eyes are bloodshot, but her smile is white and the room smells of vanilla. She has long gray hair that is almost white, her eyes a dull shade of blue. Light slips in through the sheer drapes and I pause to move them aside, looking down on the city, the placid lake to the east, the sky clear and blue. And cold. If the coffee doesn't wake me up, it's the random times I forget to warm the attachments, a cold hand screwed on sending shivers up my arm. It fractures throbbing veins all the way to my heart. What's left of it.

"Could you kiss me first?" she asks.

I nod my head.

"It's part of the package, miss. Not that you aren't pretty."

"I know what I am," she gasps, reaching for the oxygen mask, "I'm a fucking ghoul, but I used to be stunning, once." She raises a bony finger and points to a collection of photos, framed and sitting on a nearby vanity.

"You don't need me for this, you know," I say. "I mean, there are other ways."

"You come highly recommended," she whispers, sucking on the mask. "Hand me those pills, please," she says, and I oblige. I pop open the top first, and she swallows down the contests of the clear tube. I hand her the water, which she holds in a trembling hand, spilling down the front of her nightgown.

"Better?" I ask.

"Take the sheet down," she says.

I pull the sheet down and she hikes up her nightie. She is glistening as she spreads her legs, one hand on her breast, her breathing accelerating, eyes on me the whole time. I lean in and kiss her, our tongues sliding back and forth.

"I'm only forty years old," she cries, tears running down her cheeks.

I stand up and go to the suitcase. I take off my right hand, and screw on the device. It is a long fleshy thing, with various buzzing and throbbing points of contact. I turn to look at her and she smiles at me, her right hand busy between her legs.

My clothes never come off.

My right arm is moving back and forth, in and out, the buzzing and rotating filling the room with a dull hive of sweaty bees, her eyes glassing over as the drugs start to kick in. It's going to be close, a race to the end. My left hand is holding her bony fingers as she gasps and moans, closer and closer. Something inside me shatters, as she bucks and shakes, the bed wet now, her back arching as the lights dim in her wide open eyes, and she stops moving now, her arms quiet at her side, her fingers falling out of mine.

I log the entry, the deposit hitting my account with a hefty tip and I accelerate the car in a straight line, no longer looking for the curves.

BRINGING IN THE SHEAVES

EVER SINCE I was a little boy, the cornfields filled my nightmares with the sounds of rustling stalks, and the stench of something decomposing. I guess you could call it a recurring dream, the way the empty fields would fill my head with gentle hot winds and stinging scratches up and down my arms. I blame it on my younger brother, Billy—it was his idea after all, his fault. But I don't hold onto that grudge. I see the girl, Margie, every once in awhile, hanging out in front of the 7-11 or maybe down by the bowling alley. Small town living doesn't offer up many options, but back then she was one of them—today, less so.

Doesn't really matter the name of our town, they're all the same, dotted across the Midwest, filling up the middle of Illinois, long arteries of dust and despair stretching out in every direction. Bluford, Cairo, Dakota—we all worked the fields, tending to chickens, hogs, cows and the like. It was a lot of early morning chores and dark nights where we tried to kill ourselves one way or another.

My younger brother Billy, only three years my junior, he'd tag along whenever he could. Sometimes

I needed somebody to shoot hoops with on the back of the barn, or to blame the broken window on, that's how it went. He was always falling down, his simple skull filled with ideas, massive forehead constantly scratched and riddled with scabs. I didn't treat him like a simpleton, but he was definitely slow. I'd hear a thud or a slam, something creaking or snapping in two, and I'd go running for the barn, running for the tractor that kept moving into the cornfield, with nobody on top of it, as it disappeared into the unforgiving folds. A tine of a pitchfork jammed through his meaty thigh, trying to fly out of the loft into a pile of hay below. An angry raccoon disappearing down the dirt road, unwilling to be his pet, Billy's face and arms bleeding, his wide grin taut over bones that knew no failure. One dead animal or another, cradled in his arms—a hen with a snapped neck, or field mice staged around a tiny table sipping at tea, a stiff cat swung around by its tail. He didn't mean anything by it, just curious, I guess. We all are.

The girl lived down the road a bit. She was always dirty, constantly lifting her torn skirt over her head, showing off her dingy underwear to whoever would look. But she was sweet on me, sweet on Billy. Margie was a year ahead of me. She probably just wanted somewhere quiet to go where her daddy couldn't touch her, where her mother couldn't lay her dead eyes on Margie's thin arms and pale skin. So we let her come over, after school, or in the summertime. We'd pal around with her down by the creek, looking for tadpoles, or frogs to put in jars, left out on a shelf where they'd dry up and leave our room stinking of something gone foul—rotten and thick.

When she asked us to tie her up, we thought she

was joking. We were older now, sixth grade for me, about twelve, and Billy only nine. I had seen a filmstrip in class once, bad illustrations of flaccid penises, the scientific data going over my head, our stunned faces flush and embarrassed by the idea of a naked woman's body, the idea of what we were supposed to do. It was dirty. And yet, it was spectacular.

We'd seen her underwear before, it wasn't a big deal, and we weren't interested in putting our tongues in her mouth. Gross. But we had nothing else to do, so we tied Margie to a post at the back of the barn, and turned to each other, mute, as she smiled in the dimly lit space. We ignored her for a bit, leaving her to squirm, to test the knots, moaning and grunting. She was our kidnapped ransom, so we went about the barn fortifying our defense, leaning broken broom handles against the wall, our weapons, gathering shovels and baseball bats, and a lone, rusty pitchfork, still stained with a bit of Billy's blood.

Billy finally approached her and licked her face, from her chin to her eyebrow, and she giggled and turned her head away. He spit into the dirt.

"Salty," he said.

He picked up a stick and started poking her, in the belly at first, and then he raised and lowered her faded skirt.

"Billy?" I asked.

He glanced at me, then back to Margie, a dirty grin easing across his face.

"What? She started this."

Margie turned to look at me, her eyes tiny fragments of coal.

"Leave him alone, Rodney," she said, "We're just playing."

"Yeah, Rodney," my brother wheezed, bending over, and raising her skirt. "Let's see what she's got."

I crossed my arms. I wanted to see too. I glanced to the house, and it was quiet, nobody in sight. Billy held her skirt up with the stick, as Margie smiled, and took his other hand and placed it between her legs.

"Nothin," Billy said. "She ain't got nothin."

A car skidded into the yard and Billy let her skirt fall back down, and quickly untied her from the post. His face was splotchy and red, as was hers, but I was cold and pale, on the verge of throwing up.

"I better get home," Margie said. "Almost dinner."

She leaned over and kissed me on the cheek, and skipped out of the barn, into the sunlight. I wiped my face, the sticky residue of strawberry bubblegum, Billy's eyes on me, glassy and empty.

◦◦◦

It was all Billy could talk about—Margie. All summer long. I didn't see her again, not for a while, but he went looking for her whenever he could. He looked for her at the grocery store with mother, whenever we went for a ride with dad, fishing or off on some errand. He leaned out of the beat up Chevy Nova like a dog, his tongue flapping in the wind.

My father always plowed a section of the back forty, a path out into the corn, with a patch of it cleared out, like his private sitting room. There wasn't much in the space, just a rusty metal chair and a crate filled with empty beer bottles, a hole dug into the earth filled with cigarette butts and spent matches. I don't blame my father for wanting this space, somewhere away from our mother, who had an endless list of things for him to do—broken latches and busted screens to fix, buckets of paint that needed to be emptied. As far as I know, he'd just sit out there in the dark, staring up at the stars, drinking and smoking, wishing to be someplace else. Anywhere else.

On the rare evenings when the two of them would go upstairs, turning the television set up loud, hand in hand as they climbed the stairs, all giggles and fists of flesh, Billy and I would head for the fields, to sit in his chair, and stare at the sky. It was as close as we'd get to the man, as close as he'd let us get. We'd find half smoked butts and smoke them, coughing and spitting onto the ground. We'd drink the warm remnants from the bottom of the bottles and cans, sweet and sour and forbidden.

When Billy started disappearing, this was the place I went. I often found him covered in blood. He wouldn't say anything, just hold his palms up to me and grin. I'd take him back to the house and clean him up, hosing him down until he started to cry, and then I'd slap him until he shut up.

Margie started showing up again, and she and Billy would disappear into the barn. They had secrets now, would go quiet when I walked into the barn. We'd still take walks together, to the creek and into the woods, even out into the cornfields, lost and scratched by the sharp stalks and ears, hollering for each other, hiding, as we choked on the dust and the heat. Inevitably we'd end up in my father's room, lying by the chair, the walls of corn around us a fortress against the rest of the world. I only saw them kiss once, but it made my stomach curl. He was too young, I thought, and even though he was my brother, he was clueless about Margie's advances. I barely understood them myself.

I cornered Margie one afternoon and warned her off my brother. She put one hand on her hip and asked me if I wanted that attention, if her time spent with my brother was something that I'd prefer she reserve for me? I told her she was crazy, but she wasn't wrong. And on an afternoon when Billy wasn't around, she and I ended up in the hayloft, our wet mouths on each other, my stomach in knots, telling myself this was what I needed to do in order to protect my brother, my hands on her dirty, sweaty body, our tongues a slick disaster.

∽

Daddy had been on the road now for weeks. Business trip, local fair, something to do with the price of our harvest and subsidies, I didn't understand it all. I knew that the house was quiet—that we were bored to death, and I knew that the bottle of whiskey that hid above the fridge was slowly emptying as our mother sat quiet at the kitchen table.

We siphoned off part of it, and replaced it with water, disappearing into the fields when she went to sleep. We choked it down as we lay in the darkness, waiting for something to happen. When I drifted off, his hands found my neck, his knees on my shoulders—the air in my lungs disappearing into the night. He'd found out about us, Margie and me, there was nothing else to explain it. He was stronger than I remembered, his eyes bulging in his head as he squeezed on my neck, showing no sign of letting up. I finally brought my knees up, banging him in the center of his back, throwing him off of me, as air rushed back into my lungs.

"Dammit, Billy," I choked. "She's not worth it. You're too young, anyway."

"Fuck you," he murmured, looking up from the ground, the darkness swallowing our sweat and our tension.

"She's my girl," Billy muttered. "Don't touch her again."

"You'd choose flesh over blood?" I asked. "She's just some stupid whore from down the road."

"Shut your mouth, Rodney."

"I'm sure I'm not the only boy she's kissing. I told you, she's no good."

Billy lay there.

"That's for me to decide," he said.

❧

Daddy never did come back from that business trip. And that wasn't a good thing. Billy wasn't talking to me—a ghost that drifted about the property, chucking rocks at anything that moved. For three days we didn't talk, until I walked past the barn and the stench of rotten meat engulfed me.

I'd let him have the barn, somewhere to go where he didn't have to look at my face. In the middle of the sweltering barn lay a large metal bowl of cat food, dusted with white powder, and surrounding it was a ring of dead cats. Their grey tongues protruded from their tiny still mouths, as flies buzzed my head.

Billy.

I yelled for him, but he didn't answer. I headed for the cornfields as sweat pushed out of every pore.

I found him standing over Margie, her arms tied behind her, sitting in the metal chair, buck naked and crying. Billy was holding a pocketknife in his hand, looming over her, poking her skin with the sharp blade. Her whimpers were lost on the wind, but her eyes bore into me.

"Billy," I said. "Enough."

He turned to me, his jaw clenched.

"We're just playing," he said. Margie shook her head back and forth, afraid to speak, and Billy backhanded her across the face.

"Stop it, Billy," I said. "It's over, let her go."

"She came here," he said. "She took off her own clothes, she sat in the chair. This is what she wants," he whined.

"No, Billy, it isn't. You've gone too far."

"No, this is going too far," he said, leaning over the girl. I started running to him, but I wasn't fast enough. He put the blade under her left nipple, her breasts hardly anything at all. Her eyes went wide as his thumb held the tiny pink protuberance, and he sliced it clean off and flung it to the ground. She gasped, unable to scream, as blood ran down her pale skin. He looked up at me, smiling, and I was on him, and we were rolling to the ground, my fists beating about his head, the tiny blade stabbing my back, my arms, until I knocked it out of his hand. I beat him until he stopped moving, and then I stood up.

Margie was crying, snot running down her lip, blood pooling in her lap.

"It's all right, it's over," I said.

Bringing in the Sheaves

I picked up the blade and walked to her, cutting the rope that bound her trembling flesh. I knelt down and held her as she sobbed into my shoulder. Straightening up, I held her face in my hands.

"Margie, don't come back here. You hear?"

She nodded her head and quickly got dressed.

❧

With Daddy gone it didn't take much for mother to drift away too. She'd picked up a job at the local diner, and we saw her less and less. Strange men came for the harvest, and we watched them descend on the farm like locust. Billy and I didn't talk any more.

When the summer ended and a cool wind started to fill the space that used to be our family farm, I went to the barn in search of Billy, ready to bury the hatchet, to move on from these transgressions, to erase from our minds what had happened out there in the fields.

A shadow swung back and forth across the opening of the barn, the stiff bodies of the sacrificial cats long gone, but the rotten stench still remaining. I swallowed a lump in my throat and stared up at the rafters, at his still body, the rope around his neck, his purple face, and a stain of urine in the dirt below his dead body. I took a breath, exhaled, and lowered my head. It didn't have to be this way.

Or maybe it did.

DIVINING

IF YOU ASKED me today the exact moment in time that I knew Heather was wrong for me, it would have to be the night her husband was banging on my apartment door, her laughter hidden under the sheets, our bodies slick with sweat. She was the kind of girl who bent over the pool table just a little too far, her top slipping down, her bra pushing up, her skin-tight jeans hugging her hips. Her eyes told you she'd never been here before, that this was new territory, eyelashes batting, a stray dark hair tucked behind her ear. She sipped at the bottle of beer as if it was an oddity—it somehow just ended up in her mouth. Sly grins and sharp white teeth devoured glossy bruised lipstick, always wet, always whispering secrets wrapped in bourbon and mint.

It rained all week so the construction site was shut down. Hiding out at Nik's Tavern with the rest of the crew was one option, a sea of flannel and denim, stubble and cigarettes, just waiting for something to happen. I saw her come in, but paid her no attention. I was worried about the rent, the stack of bills on my kitchen table, hoping I wouldn't have to start selling pot again. My arms were mottled from donating blood, my sperm scattered all over the city. When I closed my eyes I saw apartments I knew, thin back doors that steel-toed boots could splinter, loose money hidden in mattresses, anything that could be hocked for a buck. It would stop raining soon, I knew that much. It had to.

I dealt the tarot cards out onto the table, looking for an answer to my prayers. The Fool was the one card that kept turning up, a stray dog yapping at the feet of the idealist, perched on the edge of a cliff. It was my way of meditating, getting closer to my god, a way of divining my path. A crack of pool balls from the back of the bar shattered the deep grumbling of impatient men.

"What's that?" she asked, her legs up against the table, her left hand shoved in a front pocket, the other holding tight to a bottle of beer.

"Tarot cards," I said, not looking up.

"What are they for?"

"Lots of things," I said. "Mostly, for telling the future."

"And it works?" she asked.

"Sometimes."

"I'm Heather," she said. "You shoot pool?"

∞

Her hand resting on the small of my back, we ran the table for the rest of the night. Whatever came up, whatever was offered, we took it, and won. And then we did it again. The beer kept flowing until the shots started, dark liquid that coated my mouth with licorice. The world faded away. She told me her story and I nodded my head and pictured her naked. In time, the room became empty, nobody willing to take us on. Lips snarled and noses twitched and we knew it was time for us to leave.

We were wet before we even got to my apartment, the cold rain soaking through our jeans, hair plastered to the side of our faces, her mascara running down her face, T-shirt clinging to her breasts. I didn't ask any questions about what this all meant. I simply peeled off her clothes and took every part of her body in my mouth, and held onto her, my fingers pressing red into her hips, her alabaster body crashing waves across my battered frame.

In the morning she was gone.

◦⁓◦

Money was scattered all over the floor, crumpled up fives and tens, a folded over wad that I knew was my rent money, not a single penny touched. My apartment was quiet, a chill in the air. Large raindrops beat against the glass. No work. Again.

On the kitchen table, the tarot cards were spread out in a reading like the one I'd done the night before. Across the middle, blocking the reading, was the King of Cups—a wise presence resting on a throne, a patient and understanding soul. The outcome, the last card in a line of four, was nothing but The Tower. Lightning struck the top of a tall grey building, flames and chaos, the card a montage of ruin.

I ran my hands down my chest, a smattering of bruises, and a solitary bite mark over my right nipple.

◦⁓◦

No number, no last name, she disappeared into the night. For weeks I didn't see her, the rain finally stopping, sending us back to work. Long days stretched out to make up for the weather—mud and rebar and the cold.

Every night I would stop by Nik's on the way home, and wait to see if she showed. She didn't. I put my money in the bank and told myself it was better this way. I didn't need her. I didn't want her.

She haunted my dreams.

∽

The pounding on the door was not her husband, the first time. It was Heather. I was out of bed before the bedside light filled the room, because I knew she had come back. She stood in the hallway, dripping wet again, her eyes swollen and bruised. There was blood on her lower lip and a gash across her forehead.

"He found out," was all she said.

I let her in. And she stayed.

Weeks went by.

When I was with her the world didn't matter. We hid out under the blankets, smoked cigarettes and drank. We ate Chinese food and rented movies and hid ourselves from each other. It was pathetic.

∽

The phone bill showed dozens of calls to a number in Indiana. When I called it a gruff male voice answered. Once, he mumbled her name. It was only a matter of time before he showed up on my doorstep. It was gasoline to her fire. Fists and broken glass and I dialed three digits to get us some peace and they dragged him away with a warning. Down at the station Heather filled out the paperwork, and we hoped it would do us some good.

The joint checking account was my idea. Or that's what I tell myself now. She pawned her wedding ring in order to get her stash, netting us a couple hundred bucks. I should have seen the rest coming.

The first sunny day in a week and I head to the job site filled with sunshine and daydreams. And when I come home the apartment is silent. My checking and savings have been predictably drained. There are boot prints in the hallway and laughter in my ears and I know that if I dial that number in Indiana she will answer the phone, laughter and cigarette smoke filling the air, her man sitting behind her drinking a cold beer, admiring her backside as she tucks a strand of hair behind her ear.

On the kitchen table the tarot cards sit in a pile, with one card turned over.

THE CULLING

DANIELLE STANDS AT the long mirror brushing her dirty blonde hair, tears running down her cheeks, as the rest of us sit at the table, the howling in the distance, my reassurances falling on deaf ears.

"Sweetheart, you have nothing to worry about," I say, sitting at the scarred and beaten table. The wind batters the walls of our homestead, my wife supping her porridge as the boy looks on in wonder.

"Easy for you to say, Daddy, you're not up for recognition."

Her long dress twists back and forth, dingy and torn, the same pattern over the windows, over the step stool—yellow flowers on a light blue fabric. I place the wooden spoon back in the bowl, the oats getting cold, and take a breath.

"We've been over this, honey, you have nothing to worry about. You've been a good girl, Danielle, I'm sure your slips will be very few in number. Tell her, Isabelle, tell her the truth."

My wife sets down her spoon, her eyes dark and liquid, a stuttering intake of breath. She has feared this day since our daughter was born. She has raised her right, knowing the ways the slips are placed in the locked box, the ways the neighbors look at our daughter—envious, angry and scared.

"Your father is right, Danielle. You have nothing to worry about. The Jenkins boys, those two alone should alleviate your fears. How many slips have they garnered? Ten, twenty, each? For the fire, the cattle, the girl they left for dead in the creek. Those two are certainly sleepless these past few nights."

Danielle brushes at her hair, tears continuing to run dirty rivulets down her cheeks. The fire flickers in the stone hearth, and the boy, David, chews on his spoon, all of this conversation lost on his wondering eyes. It will be years before his own culling, many moons from now.

"Jacob is a booger eater," David says, his face covered in oats. He's speaking of the Jenkins boy, the oldest. They are dirty, violent boys, who have embraced their futures with reckless aplomb. They cannot both be taken, so they roll the dice and wait.

A cracking sound outside is followed by the deep thud of branches falling to the ground and our heads turn toward it. When the winter pushes across the river, it moves with a speed that is dangerous and true. The trees are covered in ice, crystal sculptures, that shatter and disintegrate in the escalating winds.

"It's time," I say, standing up, rubbing my hands together, the walls rattling, dust and hay falling to the wooden floor, and my wife breaks out in guttural sobs.

$\backsim$

The town hall is filled and overflowing. We have walked the mile from our home at the edge of the forest, following the cart path, every bit of clothing we own worn in layers from head to toe. Danielle has refused to wear anything but her favorite dress—her only dress. These are her terms now, and I honor them.

We sit at the back of the room, heads turning back and forth, eyes running over every teenager, every unmarried boy and girl that is eligible for nomination. The wind marries with the howls of the great grey beasts that will lumber down from the mountains at daybreak, taking our offering as their own. It is a sacrifice, one that has been witnessed and accepted for as long as I have lived. We do not question it. It is our own way of thinning the herd, punishing the sinners, a cautionary tale for the rest.

Outside the bonfire has been built, a singular pole standing in the center of split wood, waiting for our nomination to be called.

"Get in there, and shut your mouth," comes a voice from the door.

All heads turn to witness Jedediah Jenkins as he corrals his boys, Jacob the booger-eater, and James, his younger accomplice, pushing them into the room. Both are dirty, spitting tobacco on the floor as they stare daggers at their pappy, blood ringing the broken nose of the oldest, the younger boy holding his right arm in pain. They have not come easily, though their bravado this past week has been unending. I forget that they are still boys, not yet men.

There are others up for nomination this year, but the Jenkins boys are the favorites to get called. Mixed in with the filth and fear are tiny groups of smiling parents, aglow with newly found wedded bliss. They have followed the rules, archaic as they may be, and have married off their daughters at the ripe old age of thirteen, to whatever boy (or man) will have them—an angry, vengeful child better than one ripped to shreds on the pike.

Andrew Pallard takes the stage, the heavy metal box sitting in front of him on a long table, the rusty lock holding it shut, a great brass key in his hand. His puffy face is flush with heat, the stress of these proceedings taking on an extra layer, as his own boy is up for nomination as well. His long coat billows around his thick frame and he turns to face the crowd.

"All eligible children please take the stage."

The room grows cold and quiet for a moment, then fills with boots shuffling, the sudden outbreak of sobbing and moaning, as parents hug their children to them, preparing for the worst.

And I see Danielle for a moment, truly see her, the beauty and fear in her blue eyes. The boy clings to my leg, and I hold my daughter to me, kiss her face, and then hand her to her mother.

"It will be okay," I tell her. "I promise."

She lets go of us and walks to the stage, standing next to the dozen or so boys and girls that now tremble, cough, and swallow their fears. Andrew turns the great wire framed drum that holds a collection of some seventy-five tiny stones. These are the callers, not the children. These are the ones that will read the slip. The bin turns around and around, the rocks beating the metal and coming to a rest, I inhale and hold my breath. When he calls my name, I exhale with relief.

I am handed the key, which I insert into the lock,

springing the box open, the slips of paper filling it, every child's name listed at least one time, the great sin of being born into this wretched, fragile world. Their eyes are on me, and they are muttering names, a babbling brook of Jenkins, Jenkins barely audible over the pounding of my heart. Andrew nods his head and steps back from the table, allowing me my moment. I reach into the box and pull out a slip and hold it up to my eyes.

Danielle Tobin.

I take a deep breath, my eyes stinging, my stomach in knots.

"Jacob Jenkins," I shout, placing the slip back into the box, as the room erupts in relief.

FLOWERS FOR JESSICA

THE DOCTORS HAD no answer for me, something wrong with her heart—that's all that I heard, all they could hint at with their stone faces and cold hands, constantly checking their watches, places they needed to be. Except, now that Jessica was gone, there was nowhere I needed to be and nowhere I wanted to go. She liked the woods, embraced nature with every fiber of her constantly distracted mind. She wandered off every chance she got—communing and dancing, her silhouette spinning in many a field of wild flowers. It gave me great pleasure to share that joy with her.

When I found her body in the deep grasses—weeds and vines bent over from the edge of the forest, she looked peaceful, asleep, hands resting on her chest. We'd been hiding from each other, playing a little game. The reward was supposed to be her soft kisses, my hands traversing her ivory skin, a stolen moment away from the city, away from the smoke and noise and drudgery of work and broken dreams. It only took a short drive north, away from our home and the echoes of lost children, the bloody rags that lined our garbage cans, the dusty crib that lay barren and quiet. I didn't bring it up any more, didn't dare ask where we were, what the plan was, or how to move forward.

Too many nights I'd find her at the kitchen table, empty glass of wine, empty bottle, her eyes a million miles away, her hands torn and bleeding, wads of paper in her mouth as she chewed, broken glass littering the table. It was a room filled with anger, a thick layer of frustration, sadness and an undying urge to hurt someone, to strike out in vengeance for the random pain that surrounded us. I'd carry her upstairs, a bundle of sticks, and place her on our bed. When she'd reach for me, catatonic, dead behind the eyes, I'd her push away. It wasn't her. Her body called to me, begged me, fill her with life, but her eyes, her diminished mind, was anywhere but here.

Fractured. That's the word that comes to mind. I can see myself in my car, drifting down the highway. I can see her at the table, a ghost. I can picture the forest, her lying in the damp green blanket of grass, and I can see what I did next in excruciating detail.

It started as a way to honor her, to hold on to her shape, her shadow, the outline of her body flattening the greenery, the death of the grasses, the weeds withering and turning brown, flower buds that had bared witness to her heartbreak, shriveled and lying on the ground. I simply lay down in her outline, lay there in the woods, the grass, and tried to imagine what she had been thinking, tried to embrace her pain and longing. Insects buzzed at the periphery of my body heat, the sun above cooking the forest, the fields, a shimmer washing over me. My body glistened with sweat, the droplets running off of my bare skin and into the earth below me. Soon my tears joined the

FLOWERS FOR JESSICA

trickle of sweat, running down the sides of my face, as I bellowed and wailed, alone in the world. Things were just beginning.

Days later, unable to focus on life in the real world, unable to be anywhere else, I returned to the forest to find the dark outline of my body, overlapping the space where she expired, filled with tiny flowers, buds of yellow and pink and lavender, pushing up from the shadows. Wildflowers. I didn't dare lie down on them, these slivers of sweetness and light. I had no water with me, no creek nearby—nothing but blue sky and a shiver in my bones.

When I returned the next day, I stopped at the edge of the clearing, sucking in air, frozen. The flowers had grown, weaving in amongst themselves, her shape appearing in the layers of green. I held in my hands an old milk jug filled with water, heavy and slick in my sweating fingers. I approached her with apprehension, wind pushing through the leaves of the forest, small creatures tangled in the undergrowth, cracking and rustling, the shrill cry of some lost and frightened bird. I opened the jug and poured it over her, over the flowers, and vines, and grasses. I traced the outline, down her head, over her shoulders, to her arms and legs and back to the top again. I created a small puddle where her brain would surely grow, another in her chest, where a heart might come to life. And then I walked away. Unsteady, I tripped over my feet, glancing back over my shoulder. My desire was uncertain.

I didn't come back the next day. Busy at work, I thought. Things I needed to do. These were the lies that I told myself, when she came to me in my dreams—in the dark. I ached for her, my hands trembling constantly, a dull throbbing at my temples. And yet, I'd lost my mind. Nowhere else to go, my vision filled with flashes of wildflowers and creeping vines, and I found myself back in the forest.

I stood at the edge of the clearing, her body expanding and contracting, her chest filling with air. She was still a shell, one glorious red rose in the center of her heart, a gathering of white buds at her head. When I summoned the courage to approach and kneel next to her, the wind picked up, whispering to me, things I needed to do. I shook my head. The trees bent under the gusts of wind, the long grasses of the field waving back and forth.

"More," it whispered. I lay next to Jessica, and the rustle of flowers and leaves as her head turned toward me—it caused my pounding heart to shudder and stop. I listened to her wishes, to the wind and the heady perfume of the wildflowers. I was weak. I stood as the sun set and unzipped my jeans and drenched the flowers and grass. There was a withering crawl of vines, the minerals and vitamins of my urine washing over her translucent skin. Nausea rolled over me and I turned and walked away. What was I doing?

Again I stayed away, fearful of what might come next. But she haunted my dreams, begged me to return, to finish the job, to bring her all the way back. I hesitated at the door to our home, several times. I'd retreat into the house and pour myself a tumbler of amber, over and over, until her voice faded into the walls. It was no use. I could not stay away.

Her final request was beyond me, and the thought of such action repulsed me. I told her it was impossible, I couldn't make lust out of wishes. Her skin was no longer translucent—it was a pale earth tone, the creeping vines still visible under her skin, the blooming rose sighing in her chest. Two violet blossoms stared back at me from her hardening skull—tracking my every move. I could see her naked form now as I stood above her, her body writhing in the grass and shadows, begging me to complete this act, to plant my seed among the other buds and seedlings that trembled at my feet. Two pink buds stood out in her chest, her right hand drifting down into the mossy growth between her legs, the wind picking up again, a hot breath at my ears, my neck, a desert of heat emerging from nowhere. I found myself aroused. As the sun disappeared into the horizon and the darkness pulled us in, I ran my hand up and down my slick flesh, a stammering in my chest, my breath caught and lost. Bountiful, she gasped and trembled, my prayers for forgiveness disappearing into the woods.

It took me a week to come back, and a part of me thought that maybe I could stay away forever. That maybe I didn't need to see this to completion, my insanity confirmed, my selfish needs and desire to see Jessica again, manifested in some horror of acts committed out of desperation. But I returned, eventually. Was there ever really any doubt?

She was lying at the edge of the forest, naked in the sunlight that pushed to the rim of the woods, her fragile silhouette disappearing in the sunbeams, reappearing in the shade. She didn't say anything when I came upon her. She didn't ask why it had taken me so long to return. She didn't question the tears that ran down my face. She opened her arms and beckoned me to her, and I knelt down, and then lay down, her arms wrapping around me, then her legs—pulling me in, pulling me under, until we were whole once again.

WICKER PARK PAUSE

IT'S THE RELENTLESS scratching at the back door that wakes me—a cat maybe, trying to get in. "Mom?" I whisper.

Even though I've started high school now, a big girl, I don't like being alone now that Dad is gone. I get out of bed wearing an old T-shirt of his, extra-large— it hangs all the way down to my knees. The dark gray material is worn and soft, and still smells a bit like him—cigars and sweat and despair.

Our bungalow is small but cozy. In the darkness, a sliver of moonlight slices through the skylight. I can see into my mother's room, the blanket pulled back, the pillow still holding the shape of her head.

There it is again, that scratching at the side door, the sliding glass door.

Mom will take care of it, she always does. She'll see what it is.

"Mom?" I say a bit louder.

My bare feet hardly make a sound on the carpet as I ease down the stairs to our living room below. I have the floor plan memorized.

Where is she? I stop at the bottom of the stairs, a shape moving around on the back patio. Across the living room the bay windows are filled with moonlight, red and tan brick and rooftops, treetops, dark sky, and in the distance the Flat Iron Building. The shape of that building has always bothered me. I've been inside it before. It has curved hallways that seem to go on forever—around every turn a different studio—a painting, raw canvas, hair and glue, and pieces of fractured metal littering the floor.

She's been tired a lot lately, Mom. Working too much. The bags under her eyes get darker each day. She is losing weight, and it doesn't look good. In the sunlight her brown eyes have a bit of yellow, her teeth always dirty as if coated in fur.

The bathroom, that's where she is. I find her there a lot these days, crying. One day, Daddy was on a business trip. The next day his clothes were packed in boxes, sitting by the front door. They went down the street to the Ark Thrift Shop without so much as a sigh. There were calls from his office, questions, but no answers. She says she doesn't know anything. I heard his voice that last night, I swear it. Half asleep, there were hushed voices and the tinkle of broken glass—a low growl in anger, a scuffle. Half awake, I felt a dull thud vibrate through the apartment, and then I fell back asleep. A dog barked next door and his voice was silenced. I don't believe he just left.

In the bathroom there is a pile of her clothes by the utility room door, just waiting to be washed. They reek of grease and cigarette smoke. In the dim light they looked torn, stained with syrup or coffee.

Garbage. She couldn't sleep so she took out the garbage. That's what it was.

A shadow passes in front of the glass. Not a cat, that's for sure.

Something falls over, metal and heavy, a crack and a squeal and something is hurt—a raccoon maybe? A dog?

I slide the door open and there is a gust of cold air, and her robe lies abandoned on the ground. It is pink and lies crumpled, as if hurt. In the alley there is the stench of garbage, something rotten and foul.

The back door slams shut and a pale figure disappears into the bathroom. I grab the robe and slide the side door shut. At the bathroom door I hear her sobbing. There is hair everywhere, as if two cats had been wrestling—dark black and grey, long and filthy.

"Mom? Is that you?"

"It's okay dear, go to bed."

"What are you doing?"

"Long story, honey, really boring."

"But, your robe . . . "

In the dark kitchen the bathroom door creaks open and her hairy hand shoots out. Long, sharp nails extend into the air, brushing my arm, the yellow tint gleaming. In a flash the robe is gone, a gasp in my chest, my breath rushing out of my body. The door shuts, with a slam and a click.

Her voice is low, barely a growl, trembling and scared.

"Go to bed, baby. Please."

ON A BENT NAIL HEAD

WE HAD A DEAL, my wife and I, and it was something we planned on keeping. Whoever went first, they'd find a way to communicate from the other side. Rebecca would often scold me, telling me with a twinkle in her earthy eyes that if I hooked up with some blonde hussy too soon after her departure that she would haunt me in every possible way. And I warned her that if she took up with one of my friends, no doubt visiting her to provide comfort in her time of need, that I'd do the same. These were the jokes we made with each other, because we were young and had no fear. We were eternal.

The woods that stretched out for miles behind our starter home, they held a darkness that would creep into our yard, over the faded fence, trying to steal our candlelit laughter. The concrete slab would hum with the language of crickets, cars rushing by in the distance, tires meeting the road, busy people off on important errands. And we'd sit in the fading light sipping cold beers that huddled in a bucket of ice, our skin sun-kissed, arms tired from labor in the flower garden, swimming at the local pool, from grasping each other tight with slick flesh and lips pressed together.

We talked of children quite often. We'd left the city and driven north all because a woman was raped in the alleyway behind our apartment. It changed the way we wandered the streets at night, restaurants full of glowing candles and the smell of garlic, glasses clinking as the city grew drowsy with sleep. It was no longer a community, no longer a place where you gave a head nod to the dreadlocks, uttered a greeting to the tattooed arms, grinned at the soul patch, ear buds filled with drum kicks and bass guitar beats. It took one look from Rebecca, coming home from work on the Blue Line el train, her dress shoes in a bag, sneakers on her feet, tight skirt wrapped tight around her curves and motion, one look from her and I knew it was over. We had to move.

She walked past me into the kitchen, pulled the cork out of a bottle of red wine, and drank it straight from the bottle.

"Honey, you okay?" I asked, turning away from the computer, jeans and boots, flannel shirtsleeves rolled up to the elbows.

"Am I fine?" she asked, one hand on her hip, an eyebrow arched. She rubbed at her collarbone, at the tiny indentation where her throat began. A sigh filled her up, her hand caressing a silver locket that had once belonged to her grandmother.

The room was fading, shadows pushing out of the corners, draping over the furniture of our tiny one-bedroom apartment. A frying pan sat on the stove, sausage grease, peppers and onions, the faint tinge of something going rancid. She turned away from me and walked toward the bed down the back hall, unzipping her skirt. The door slammed and the room eased into a wash of darkness. No, she wasn't fine at all.

❧

Six months we'd lived in the new house, two miscarriages under our belts. So we stopped. Not just the sex, the trying, we stopped being who we were, a couple. We became instead, two bodies that passed each other, floating on water that was slick with oil, bumping into each other with muttered apologies and blinking eyes. I kept telling her we were young, that it was okay, it wasn't her fault—there was nothing to be upset about. She ate my words and swallowed them down, vomiting into the toilet late at night, her anger, and anxiety laced with wine and cigarettes and hatred.

So I started leaving her notes, when I went to work. I was only waiting tables, nothing special, but I hated to leave her alone. She kept calling into work, sick she said, her panties dotted with blood. They gave her time, the office would be there, they knew about the rapist, they knew about her body failing her, and they were not yet fed up with her rain clouds and sneers.

The notes were physical manifestations of my growing desperation, and I made sure they came from my voice, an adult. I didn't want her to think I was playing games with her, sing-song nursery rhymes from our now dead offspring transcending space and time. I signed them too. Always love, always and forever. I told her I loved her, unconditionally. There was a bouquet of flowers, just through the gate, and down the path, to where the dirt became a fork in the woods. But she had to get up and go get them.

When I came home late that night, the house was quiet, a thin sheen of electricity, and a bouquet of flowers on the kitchen table, a faint smell of roses and lavender offering us some peace. I took in a breath, and headed for the bedroom where I pressed my body against her quiet frame, and held her tight for just a moment.

She went back to work. But the notes continued. Back and forth they went. Waking up, my arms aching from carrying trays of food, a small card of peach stock sat folded on the kitchen table, leaning against the vase. So I ventured into the woods. The edge of the dirt path seemed as if it had been swept, but I smiled and shook my head, surely imagining these things. At the fork in the road a single nail was pounded into a hearty oak, and on a piece of string a small package dangled, wrapped in light blue paper, twisting in the faint, flowery breeze. I took the loop off the nail and opened the present, a crimson candle sat squat in thick glass, a musky scent of sandalwood and red currant. We used to light this candle in the city, and the thick sweetness would fill our tiny bedroom, our bodies always willing and draped over each other, lips and teeth and immersion. When she came home from work I was waiting upstairs in our bedroom, the candle burning, lying on the bed, and she slipped out of her clothes without a word. In the echo of the fading evening her moans became sobs, and I held her, and told her everything would be okay. We fell asleep early that night, the darkness pulling us under.

I bent the nail head trying to hammer it back into the scarred flesh of the tree, trying to tie a bottle of red wine to a string that kept pulling the metal out of the tree. I laughed to my invisible audience, leaves rustling and branches snapping, the distant sounds of suburban life like a television show turned way down low.

The path to the giving tree was now dotted with yellow dandelion heads. The path to the tree now had a trail of votive candles, blinking in and out, in the sighs of the watching forest. And we were trying again. Trying to make a family.

$\sim$

We didn't talk about it, it wasn't three months yet, that was the superstition we had to embrace. You don't say you're pregnant. You don't get too excited. We'd been down this path before. Three months, we had to wait. And every time she got up to go to the bathroom, every time she shrieked over a spider, I thought we'd lost out yet once again. So we smiled and held hands at the dinner table, we ate meatloaf and mashed potatoes, and we stared at the forest, the one tree that stood at the fork in the road, and wondered if we should still be honoring the shrine. It was getting cold out now, it could start snowing at any time. Or it could just be frigid for months. We burrowed in, we hunkered down, a fireplace filled with licking flames, and the couch swallowing us up as we held on to each other, voices silent.

Four months. Five months. Six months, and still, we kept our mouths shut. She was starting to show. We kept our secret. Always and forever, we said. Until death do us part.

Every time that I came home from work and found an empty house, I lost my breath and stalked the encroaching face, waiting for the inevitable, waiting for the other boot to drop. And then I'd find her asleep in our bed. Or I'd find a note saying she was out with friends. Or I'd check the voice mail, she was working late, hiding her bump, afraid to say anything out loud.

I went out to the tree and tied a tiny cross that I'd made out of twigs to the bent nail head that leaned rusty against the bark. The woods were silent and unresponsive.

⌒

Pulling on my leather coat, I hopped into my sensible beige sedan and drove home, late. I was tired and greasy and tense. As I pulled up into the driveway, the phone started buzzing. I pushed on the brake as the garage door opened, the screen filling up with numbers and light—one message, two messages, twelve messages. I pushed open the car door and dashed into the garage, her shiny black ride quiet in the night. I pushed open the door and dashed into the kitchen, yelling her name—Rebecca, Rebecca.

On the kitchen floor was a slick of red, turning brown on the hardwood floor. A rug by the sink was pushed to one side, black heel marks skidding across the wood, a plate on the kitchen table, empty except for crumbs, a glass of milk nearly empty, red lips ringing the rim. And the quiet—so much quiet.

I listened to the messages, first from Rebecca, then from the doctor. And then I drove to the hospital, numb.

It was suffocating, the family, the friends. They filled every corner of my house, and I wanted to yell at them, tell them to leave, to just leave me alone and get out. And every time I opened my mouth, my brother would wrap his arms around me, and hold me until I couldn't speak. The eyes would dance over me and I'd look away, reaching for whatever bottle I could find, and repeatedly, they'd vanish from my fingertips, until the house was finally empty, my brother asleep on the couch, my parents long dead, her family gone at last, and the last thing I remember is the shine of the silver locket lying on her pale neck, her eyes closed, and the whole weight of it all dragging me under.

At some point in the middle of the night, her elbows push into my sides and I wake up to an empty bedroom, the taste of bourbon on my lips, thirsty and disoriented, a headache looming at the edges of my skull. I stand naked in the room, the layout of the house that never became a home, unfolding in front of me, silently down the carpeted stairs, slipping out the back door, the cold air slapping my skin. The back gate is open, my feet turning to slabs of concrete, as I stumble down the dirt path, a dull glow of the moon overhead helping to light the way. I pause at the fork in the road, and swinging in the black air, a silver locket on a chain, her necklace left for me in the ever-expanding woods, swinging back and forth.

And I know that Rebecca has kept her word.

DANCE, DARLING

TO SEE THEM in the grocery store, with their hair all pinned up, their faded grey suits freshly pressed and their red lipstick blazing, they were somebody's grandmothers, eyes twinkling, hushed conversations over grapefruit and green onions, their secrets buried deep. But if you looked close, there were hints of something more—faded ink on both of their wrists, concurrent numbers of 140603 and 140604. If you watched them fill up their grocery cart, you'd have to look close, for the bottle of cheap bourbon nestled in between heads of lettuce and bags of hard candy. The prescription bottles were quickly shuttled into their leather purses, a quick smile to the pharmacist, no eye contact between them, the nightmares that would come later that night still hours away. They wouldn't talk about it in the daylight, Lucy with her blonde wig hiding the radiation treatments, the cancer long gone, but the shadows and screams still right around the corner. They talked about very few things that mattered in the daylight, Darcy chain-smoking, her dry skin like faded parchment, her bloodshot eyes always rimmed with tears, pushing the cart across the linoleum, one wheel rattling out of sync.

The boys would help them to the car, sunshine on

them like a searchlight, a moment in each of their tiny bird hearts where their ribcages rattled, wings fluttered, and the echo of gunshots caused them to stutter a step, grab the young man by the bicep, and gasp in hushed voices—curses muttered to the hot tar of the parking lot below their clumsy feet. They apologized, always, but the boys didn't mind. The sisters were part of the history of the store, always together, never just one. They tipped one dollar and only one dollar, whether it was a grocery cart overflowing with toilet paper and family size bottles of aspirin, or a bag of apples, fresh from the local orchards. Nobody knew if their last name was actually Cipher, because they always paid in cash, never with a credit card, never revealing that little bit of history. And when Lucy and Darcy pulled out of the parking lot in the long Cadillac, something out of the 1970s, a car that Johnny Cash might drive—black death stretched out forever, their wraparound sunglasses comical on their withering faces—the boys would wave, and pause for a moment. For under the floral perfume was a hint of something sour, something going bad.

It wasn't much of a choice, the dancing, the games they had played, the roles they fulfilled. They told each other, over rocks glasses splashed with amber liquid, ashtray overflowing, the sun setting behind torn blinds and faded drapes—that they had no choice at all. They were children then, five years old—too young for labor, nearly worthless in the eyes of the pale demons that descended on the captives with random acts of violence and hatred. As twins they were oddities, special, but only in their deviation. The gas chambers were always there, a threat that was never empty, faces they knew constantly disappearing, their parents long gone, the screams of their mother like talons over their cold, white skin, slicing them open—the dead eyes of their father two dark orbs that would float in the night sky for eternity. They shut down, Lucy and Darcy, the tears that flowed only drawing more attention, the rough hands of the guards eager to shake them, to bark orders at those that stood around them. "Schweigen," they would yell, "Schweigen die kinder." Silence the children. So they went mute.

Years. A lifetime expired. And yet, they survived, the sisters. Not without effort. Darcy in a bathtub, the razor long and eager to nip, her forearm opened up as a sacrifice, the numbers carved out and left floating on the surface of the crimson water. Lucy learned first that they were now inseparable—always within earshot, always a head cocked listening for the silence that meant success had been achieved, death recognized with a loving embrace. No, not on her watch, she'd mutter. And when she finally could hold Darcy up no longer, sinking into her own darkness, a needle and a spoon, it was her arm that begged to be broken, severed, stabbing at the fading ink that branded her skin, numbers that reminded her of what she was—a commodity, a piece of meat, something to be sorted, stacked and put on a train to a distant land. As if hearing a noise that only a twin can hear, Darcy appeared in the doorway, out of breath, her waitress apron still on, her fast hand slapping bare skin, Lucy trembling and crying out in anguish, the open hand coming again and again, across her face, knocking her to the floor, snapping the syringe in half, holding her as they collapsed to the floor.

The men knew they were damaged, but they filled the room anyway, lined the stage, as the Cipher Sisters danced. It made no sense, the dancing. It triggered hazy memories of phonographs spinning, glasses clinking, men in dark uniforms, fires blazing in stone hearths, women in pearls laughing the death laugh of survival, hands on shoulders, lips at ears, hems rising up in an effort to coerce. "Tanzen, lieblings," the women would say, settling in whatever lap was free, the men like wolves with their teeth bared, hair bristling beneath their caps, skulls trembling with dark deeds. Always together, the rooms lined with mirrors, the stages ringed with dull bulbs, holding each other up, pushing each other down, as the dirty money fell to the stage floor, wadded up, folded in half, tucked in garters and gathered with shaking arms. They were lost. Backstage they would find each other again, pick up the pieces, filling their handbags with rent money, whispers and cigarette smoke, empty pint bottles dropped into garbage cans. "Dance, darlings," Darcy would chuckle, "If only for a moment."

They filled a library with black and brown leather journals, wall to wall and floor to ceiling. They put it all down, in excruciating detail, never sharing, never reading, just channeling the darkness, vomiting out the suffering, in an effort to rid themselves of the poison that had seeped into their bones. On a good day they would smile at each other over grapefruits and green onions, knowing they were broken, knowing that it was futile, but unable to surrender, not now. They would place bent hands with swollen knuckles on the shoulders of the boys and the world would not crush them. And on the way home—the long, black car slicing the sunshine, prowling the back streets, a predatory grin in polished chrome, their only defense against the shadows that followed them—they would stop at the railroad tracks as the gates fell down, as the lights flashed and the whistle blew, hand shooting out to grasp for each other, smiles pasted on their faces, ignoring the cattle cars that flew by, the faces staring out, the screams never ending, and they would cry quietly in the black car, and say nothing—not a word.

Fractured, worn out, the library full, the refrigerator empty, stomachs tied in knots, they would lie down on the king sized bed they shared, and close their eyes. The papers would say they died within weeks of each other, but that was a lie. As if sharing the same breath, Lucy and Darcy listened to the phonograph that looped over and over, and they held each other, apologies whispered, until they could hold each other no longer. They let each other go, hands at their sides, wrists scarred with pink mottled tissue, their efforts in vain, ciphers no more.

THE FIX-IT MAN

THERE IS NO way for a middle-aged man to stand outside a grade school playground, stubble on his face, stinking of cigarette smoke and bourbon, without drawing unwanted attention. Leaning against the cold wire fence, fingers pushing through the thin worn gloves, the wind would pick up and cut through my clothes, no matter how many layers I wore. I would stare across the pavement for as long as I could, watching the games they'd play, the tag and the inevitable screams, the girls with their rosy cheeks, the boys with scowls of determination. Not for long, no, I never had much time to enjoy them, their innocence and freedom. I could feel their eyes on me, the teachers, the women, and I'd quickly move on. They had their theories, and they were wrong.

It wasn't his fault, the boy—it was always my own undoing. I wouldn't claim me either.

I liked to make things, with my hands. I'd sit in the basement, the concrete walls dusty and gray, and inhale the airplane glue, working on the models, taking needle and thick thread to a decapitated doll, springs and gears pushed inside the toys and watches, sipping amber liquid. I let her drift away, my wife, I stopped trying—and that was the beginning of the end. She was all that was right in the world, and I was nothing but regret. When the friendship is over, when the two of you can hardly be in the same room together, when the idea of sex is not only a novelty but a growing repulsion—then something inside you dies. And in that death, a universe is born.

I grew fat and lazy in my retirement. Years at the factory bent over the conveyor belt, it took a toll. Doesn't matter what I made, does it? Computer motherboards, ink cartridges, belts, tires—they all sucked me dry. I was hunched, crooked, and devoid of emotion—my head stuffed with cotton. When the time came, I tumbled into the machinery, bent and broken, but still alive. One more failure stacked on a pile of other failures. She was not surprised.

In the dark basement, a solitary light bulb overhead, the joint of my left arm itching, always itching, where the pins pushed up against the bones, buried deep inside the scarred and pitted flesh, I waited for an epiphany, a way out of the mess I had created. I counted the hours until my wife would slam the door shut, and drag our son with her, out into the world. He was better off with her, away from me. The boy wouldn't come down here now, not unless I invited him, not unless his mother was standing there in the tiled kitchen, coffee burning, arms crossed, her nose twitching like a coke-addled rabbit. Not even with my own son—she trusted me as far as she could throw me. All I had ever done was provide far less than she needed, in every possible way.

This was the ghost I had become, hiding in the shadows, my dreams trapped in the filament of shrunken spider webs—wriggling, struggling—but still alive. The shell of a man became a specter at the playground, at his soccer games, where I was invisible, barely worth a nod of the head and a painful grin. She never acknowledged me, my wife. Nor did the boy. But I was there. The other parents avoided my failure like a virus they could catch.

I would laugh. And then I would catch myself, realizing that a dirty, damaged, laughing man was not the person you wanted to be. Too many times the police suddenly appeared, too many times pushed up against a brick wall—handcuffed, abused and beaten for no reason. They would look at my driver's license, I would explain in hushed tones, and they would scowl at me, the young cops blushing, realizing they had just roughed up a drunken cripple, a man who lived just a few blocks away in a nice little house, on a quiet suburban street. I was not the boogeyman—not one of them, the unknown, but one of us—the known, the safe—homogenized. The fear in their eyes asked me how the fall had happened, how I came to be so lost— the mystery of it tense and unsettling. Could this darkness find them as well?

I started leaving the toys and dolls on the bench outside the school or tied to the fence—hidden in the brick corners of a building that held inside it children made of newly fallen snow. In my own house I was a shadow, amorphous—no more kisses at bedtime, no more stories to be read—just a darkness that in time would move on—a stain to be cleaned, a demon to be expelled. I knew it was coming, the phone calls, the hushed whispering—so maybe I'd make it that much easier. Maybe I'd hurry this whole thing along.

The things I fixed, the totems, the toys—they had

been thrown away, broken, and now I had made them whole. I would lace one arm of a cloth doll through the wires of the fence, and then the other, just high enough off the ground so the kids could find them. Or simply leave a model airplane sitting on a bench, a tree stump, on top of a garbage can, as I shuffled down the street to an abandoned gas station, surrounded by gears that no longer turned, pumps that had run dry, the architecture a skeleton of past mistakes. It was all I could do to stay in touch with the realities that were slowly slipping away.

On the final day of my freedom I sat weeping on a bench at the edge of the playground, as my son approached me and took my gnarled hands in his own. I didn't even have to commit the crime, only look as though I had. Santa Claus outside of a mall is just a drunk fat man who puts children on his lap—and that, my friend, will get you arrested. Doesn't matter if it's true.

"Dad, are you the one making the toys? Fixing them?"

I nodded my head.

"Why are you crying?" he asked.

He climbed onto my lap, smiling up at me with wide eyes, his only wish that I would smile and stop crying, be happy once again.

"No, son, don't—run along," I said.

But my boy didn't count, his vote was worthless, it was the others, the ones that ran across the playground in fear, not caring, not understanding, as I drifted into the fractured grey sky— my son, my life, slipping away. All it would take would be one scared little girl, brow beaten into submission, afraid of the strange man, the gifts he had given, nodding her head about things that had never happened, just to make them stop. I was counting on it.

And I would not be denied.

GANDABERUNDA

WHEN RODNEY FOUND the tiny bones scattered on the concrete slab that was his front porch, he assumed they were from a small animal, like a raccoon or a squirrel. In time, he learned that he was wrong. When the long shadows passed over the back yard, and a gust of cool wind caused the skeletal branches of the skinny dogwood tree to bend and wave, he hardly glanced up, thinking airplane, in his fearless skull—airplane, airplane, airplane. When the phone started ringing at all hours of the night, his mother's voice rising to a high pitch, he rolled over and went back to sleep, because death had never visited their doorstep before. He had no base of knowledge.

There were cops at his school the next morning, Rodney noticed, as the beige 4-door crept up to the parking lot. His mother drove him as usual, but today she walked him in—all the way in. She nodded to Mr. Langer, the gym teacher, with his bushy mustache and crossed arms, a hairy beast guarding the door to Rodney's school. His mother held his hand, and it was nothing new—he liked to hold his mother's hand, his father's hand, they felt large and warm—safe was the word that came to mind.

The classroom would have an electric quality to it all day long, as rain beat at the windows like knuckles—knocking and knocking, wanting to come inside. Rodney noticed that Millicent was missing. She was his very first crush. It would make the day slower, the math problems dry and calculated, no dishwater blonde across from him with a smile and a toss of her hair. There would be tears in the hallway later that week, anguish echoing in the hallways. But Rodney would be long gone by then.

Hushed voices in the kitchen, and Rodney sat on the couch, a juice box in one hand, and a bowl of Cheetos by his side. The puppy lay next to him, eyes to the ground, and then back to him, her black tail wagging furiously, and then stopping. Her head kept lifting to look at the mother, to look at the father. There was whispering in the kitchen, words that Rodney didn't understand, exhaled with a heavy despair. Abduction was one of them—pedophile another. His parents were also wrong. The bones from the other day flashed across his mind's eye, but Rodney pushed the image away. Stupid bones. They meant nothing to him, not sacrifice, or remains, they were not real—they were not familiar at all.

The puppy ran around the back yard, yapping at the leaves that fell from the neighbor's oak tree, faster and faster in an infinite loop, around the swing set, around Rodney as he stood in the breeze, his mother watching from the kitchen sink, the sun setting over the faded wooden fence. He stared at the sky—and with Halloween approaching—the myths and fables came back to him. He thought of wolves and huntsmen, he thought of sharp teeth at his neck. He laughed and lowered his eyes to the dog, a black shadow blurred across the dying grass. When the wings expanded overhead, the leathery skin taut across ancient bones, he opened his mouth, to scream perhaps—and then he was gone.

SHACKLED TO THE SHADOWS

THE DARKNESS WRAPPED around them like a blanket, the silhouettes of the campers a line of totem poles facing inward toward the flames. In the distance a lone train whistle cleaved the night, its echo turning into the baying of wolves, the rustle of the tree leaves a hesitant applause. It was his turn now, Damon, to take the dare or speak the truth. He'd been waiting a long time for this, his confession a weight that had been pushing down on him for as long as he could remember.

"You want to know?" he asked, wringing his hands as he sat on a stump, the sparkling eyes of his friends and enemies darting to him and then away. He was a tall kid, skinny and awkward, with fingers that extended down over his knees, as he tapped his bouncing legs, licking his lips, unsure. His long black hair had been recently shaved, a rash just barely visible under the stubble that dotted his pale head.

"The truth? You want the truth?" He laughed into the cold air, twigs popping in the bonfire, a soft breeze pushing through the woods as his dark eyes started to glaze over with a translucent film.

"Why not. Why the fuck not," he said. "You'll all forget me, anyway. I'll go back to the shadows, the edge of every conversation, every gathering—laughter on lips and hands on hips and Damon . . . that weird kid from down by the park. His mom's a whore, you know, his dad's a pedophile. None of that shit is true. My mother's a nurse and my dad works for the railroad—they go to church every Sunday and wonder how the hell I fell so far from their saintly goddamn tree. Soon, they'll forget me too," he said, staring up into the overhanging branches of the trees. "It'll be like I was never here," he whispered to the night.

Damon ran his teary eyes over the crowd that ringed the fire, as their heads bowed down to the flames, flashes of orange and red—flickers of something transforming—heat and tension and guilt.

"You brought me here," he said. "All of you did, with your actions and failures."

Pale moonlight washed over the treetops and Damon spoke to their fears, the lonely moments in the middle of the night when each and every one of them had stared holes into their ceilings, sweating out their betrayals, begging for forgiveness—praying to be overlooked.

"Molly Anderson, such a sweet woman. She makes the best chocolate chip cookies, always there for the football games, or the corn and pork roast at Saint Mary's. She's also got quite a mouth on her. Her and Amy Avila love to chat once their husbands have gone off to work, gossiping and criticizing over coffee and blueberry muffins. Molly just couldn't wait to tear her husband down—Barry, that fleshy, innocent bastard. On a cold Monday she raised her upper lip and went on and on about his lack of passion in the bedroom, selling his manhood short several inches, his prowess assigned to the minutemen of the American Civil War. She pulled up her shirtsleeves to show bruises, gasps filling the white kitchen as the clocks ticked on and her lies began to fester. Barry wouldn't hurt a fly—the marks were from her Tae Kwon Do class, where she fantasized about screwing her instructor, coming home to masturbate in the shower, angry at the hand that life had dealt her. And while he was no animal in the sack, Barry's cock was just about average, his lovemaking satisfactory. The only time he'd ever raised his hands to Molly was to give her a hug and tell her to have a good day. Later that night I stood over the mouthy bitch and let my hands rest on her stomach, her eyelids twitching, a soft moan escaping her lips— the pea that was growing inside of her shriveling to a wrinkled clot that would pass between her legs, her sobs on the toilet like a wounded barking dog. She would mutter to herself, asking why, what had she done, fearing her actions had brought this punishment to her. And she was right."

Damon rubbed his temples with his bruised fingertips, closing his eyes for a moment. A snake of tension uncoiled in his gut, as his flesh started to slip and fade, the blood in his veins showing through his skin, his fingernails loosening—he'd said too much already.

"Andy Pettis, big man on campus, zipping around town in his red Mustang, letterman's jacket on, music blasting and not a care in the world. Except, he liked to give certain ladies a ride home—blonde angels wearing tight jeans and blue eyeliner. Not just any girls, only the ones that were dating his friends. He had a thing for taken women, the ones that said no until they finally said yes. As they unzipped their painted-on pants, and slipped down their panties, as they unhooked their bras and sucked on his hard cock it wasn't the physical beauty of these women that turned him on, it was getting one over on his buddies, taking what was theirs, showing the world he could do whatever he wanted, that there would be no consequences for his actions. I started with slit tires, but he only bought new ones, never feeling the danger that was barreling his way. I stood over the loose dirt at the forest preserve, listening to the angry whispers of Andrea Dooling as she cursed the boy from her fresh grave, an echo of refusals, one after another, until her voice was finally quiet—her head and heart seeping out into the trembling soil. I stood on the overpass and waited for him to drive under, the smell of oil and freshly cut grass, the blinding headlights a herd of possessed horses as the cinder block fell from my hands. Had he been drinking? Sure. And what's one more bit of concrete in a heap of twisted metal and broken glass. They'd leave his Mustang on the front lawn of the high school for months after his death—a warning to the other kids to toe the line and behave themselves. And around his grave there were dozens of blonde angels, crying into their boyfriend's shoulders. I wrote down their names as I leaned against an aging crypt. The dark cloud descended over Andy's parents, his little sister clinging to the long legs of her father—I could tell that my work there was done."

Damon blinked his eyes and took a shallow breath,

the smell of burnt flesh filling his nostrils, as whispers of smoke rose from his head.

"Jasper Williams, science teacher, and recluse—except in one part of town, over by the Humane Society, where he was something of a God. He had rescued so many animals over the years—aging German Shepherds that could hardly walk, fat tabby cats in orange or gray stripes—taking them home so they wouldn't be put to death. But the funny thing about Jasper is that if you looked at his kitchen table, as I have, you'd see an ever-expanding stack of mail. Dozens of envelopes that were never opened, from animal hospitals and clinics, urging Jasper to come see them as soon as possible—overdue; annual; required by law stamped in red. Snowball and Champ, Sally and Sadie—Squiggles and Rusty and Quixotic—time for their rabies shot, time for their physical, new flea and tick medicine to be bought. No, Jasper wouldn't be bringing in the fluffy Maine coon or the sad-eyed beagle. Jasper was a man of science, and in his basement there were cold, metallic tables littered with syringes and scalpels, the stench of urine filling the air. His shaking hands would squeeze the life out of one animal after another, crying as he did it, begging for forgiveness, trying to appease the dark gods that made him do such things. In Jasper's world, this was a stopgap measure—a release, a tamping down of his rotten desires. When I fed him to the gray sows out past the cornfields, down the dusty dirt road and out past the dying trickle of a creek, it was one appendage at a time, one glistening organ after another, with a gleam in my eye. Jasper was never going to amount to very much, never make it to the big leagues. His potential had been fully realized, a waste of my time.

"This isn't God's work I'm doing," Damon said, "this leaking chaos, this black disease that I've been spreading."

The woods had gone silent, just the popping of the wood in the fire, the shuffling of feet in the dirt, eyes glancing up and then down, waiting for a punch line, sucking down cold beer, and searching their memories for their own dark deeds.

"It's not my fault, you realize that, right?" Damon asked, to a silent response. "I exist because of you. I don't want to be here. I've been shackled to the shadows for too long now, let me go!" he yelled, fists clenched in rage.

Somewhere in town a brother replaced his sister's birth control pills with unflavored baby aspirin—angry with her for growing up too fast, and leaving him behind. Somewhere in town a mother slapped her infant son, the child falling to the ground in tears and a flushed confusion, peeing into his diaper as a tiny knot of blackened flesh knitted around his pounding heart. Somewhere in town a father watched his daughter change her clothes, the bedroom door open a crack, waiting for the right time, waiting for her to develop just a little bit more, sitting in his recliner with the ballgame on, and a twinkle in his eye.

Damon flickered in the fading light of the fire, a gust of wind pushing smoke in his direction—and he disappeared.

"So, who wants to play truth or dare?" a voice asked.

PLAYING WITH FIRE

THE WOLVES DON'T come out during the day. It's something that took me a long time to figure out. I would hide in the daytime and then cower in the darkness, high up in a massive oak tree as they ran in circles beneath me. How could I get anything done? How would I survive? Before I knew of their existence, and they knew of mine, I wandered the island without a care in the world, my arms filled with seashells and driftwood—and handfuls of fruit from the orchard by the caves. But then they found me. And I was willing to let this be the end. But when the night fell, and the owls hooted from the edge of the forest and the fireflies danced at the edge of the field, I remembered that I did care—that I still loved Isabella. Against all that was holy and pure, I wanted to see her again, to hold her in my arms and nuzzle her neck, to feel her lips on mine, her arms around me—our glossy flesh melting into an eternal, liquid enlightenment.

And yet, I lived in fear of her return.

There are things we whisper into a pillow at night, simple requests. Take me, not her. Give me her pain, I can take it. Some prayers are better left unanswered.

The land was still empty then, the rest of the world just down the road, not under water. There was an endless supply of meat and water, a store for every item I needed, each tool for the job that I wanted at hand. That was then. We are all trapped here now, on this parcel. The hairy beasts, the hooting owls, the google-eyed rats, the shadows in the caves—none of us can escape.

I was not prepared.

The research, my dead wife, the disease that tore down the trees and the fruit, the vanishing that slowly worked its way across the land—it was a lightning bolt from the sky and a slow seeping through a frayed, layered bandage. I went to sleep in a canvas tent, and woke up to an ocean of black reflections. For the work I did, there were wrenches and hammers, spikes and shovels, nets and tape. It was a finite and laughable stock of goods, a treasure chest that I would treat as holy manna.

On the day that I made the saw, the day that I stood on this hill, no roof over my head, no walls to keep the animals away, I asked for many things.

First, I asked for the rain to stop. And it did. And then I prayed for strength.

When it stopped raining and there was nothing in sight, no roads off into the distance, the farmlands and prairies gone for as far as I could see, the lone piece of land that stood up to the onslaught—that was where I stood.

I couldn't be alone. There must be others—even if I was dead inside.

The tent had been torn apart and sucked up into the wind on the third day after the flood. I huddled against the sheer rock face that lead up to the caves, unable to get there. As the lightening cracked the sky and the moon hung over it all heavy and somber, I stared at the woods that surrounded me and came up with an idea. I had to build a shelter, a cabin, and I had to build it fast.

The wing of the plane. The wing.

I took that wing apart one panel at a time, struggling to get to the long strip of sheet metal, one piece about six feet long, in order to build the saw I needed. I spent the first day with a wrench and a hammer, loosening the bolts, unhooking the metal, trying to get at the raw sheet that was no longer going to fly anywhere. I flayed my fingertips and cursed the bloody metal. I slowed down, bandaged my fingers, and went back at it again.

In time I freed the metal, and started to cut in the blades. First I went over it with a black magic marker that I found in the cockpit of the plane. Then I traced over the black line, the jagged teeth as big as my palms, back and forth, tracing over and over, with the tip of a long, silver screwdriver. I didn't have any tin snips, no garden sheers, not even a pair of scissors. I traced this line as the screwdriver gouged into it, slowly curling away strips of the metal.

It was an eternity.

Maybe this was hell.

If I focused on a singular line, back and forth, back and forth, I could see my progress, the line deepening, the indentation pushing through the metal. When it looked like I had gone far enough, I bent the metal back and forth, back and forth until it snapped.

It went on like this for some time. Days. I kept walking back to the caves, staring up at them, nestled into the wall, resting under the shadow of the oak trees, the open fields unsettling to me. At night I would climb up into its branches.

I stopped keeping track of it all. I knew what lay in front of me, the wood. At some point the last blade popped loose and I had the saw in its rough form. Now, it needed to be sharp.

I scoured the beach for rocks, anything that looked like it could hold up to the blade, the raw metal, and carried them back to the hill. I ran them across the edge and the metal started to shine. The black rocks from down by the waterline, they seemed to hold up the best. But it was tricky. They would dissolve over time, once I got a groove started, leaning just this way and that, waiting for the moment when the metal pushed through and ran its fresh teeth across my flesh. It only had to happen one time, in order for me to understand. Eventually the blades were sharp.

I ate the fruit that I discovered down by the orchard, it looked safe to me, untreated by disease. I thought of Isabelle with every bite, the look on her face when she became swollen with the rotting sickness, trying to forget the way that she expanded.

I set out whatever buckets and tubs I could find.

Then, I prayed for it to rain.

∽

Down on the beach I pull my boat up on the shore and drop it into the hot sand. I am at the south end, searching for driftwood, to add to the fire pit behind the hut. There is plenty today, some of it worn smooth from the water, other pieces fractured on the rocks. I fill up my arms and take it back to the hut, dumping the wood into the pit.

It is a dull indentation in the earth, nothing more than a vessel for fire and ash. And yet, the flames have always flickered hypnotically. Easy to fall into them, their heat and lashing tongues, easy to forget the darkness around me.

Later in the day I stumble across a downed tree at the edge of the small forest that rings the caves. Broken off from the rest of the oak is a massive limb, three or four feet around, and I vow that it will be part of my home. It is not as rotten as the rest of the tree, still solid enough in its six feet of length to resist my every effort to move it. I lift one end and tug at it, pulling it ever so slowly, the hind end gouging out the soft soil, my back straining under the weight.

Each day I walk to the shadow of the caves, staring at the rocky sheer, looking for handholds, eyeing the cracks and imagining the climb. I envision my certain cold plummet, hands slipping, knees barking off of the stone. If only I could be sure that my spine would be severed, my neck snapped, then maybe I would try to climb to the caves. I was not yet desperate enough to feel the sharp teeth of the wolves on my skin, tugging, tearing, as I lay beneath them, paralyzed from the fall, but awake to witness their unchecked hunger.

I have an idea.

I untie the rope that hangs from the front of the boat, and take it with me off to the limb. If I can find a way to distribute the weight, maybe I can pull this log to my home. From the plane wreckage just north of the woods I snag the last of the in-flight blankets.

I lay the small blue blanket at the top of the log, and

roll the massive timber on to it with a shove and trembling legs. A tear at the top of the blanket is quickly torn even wider, separating the cloth with a slow and painful rip. I tie the loose ends of the blanket around the thick rope, over once, and then again, in a handmade knot that I am certain will not hold. And then I throw the rope over my shoulder. I dig my heels in and slowly lean forward, the fibers digging into my shoulder, my hands gripping the rope with every ounce of strength I can muster, and I slowly began to walk forward.

It is slow—my back strains against the weight of the log. It has to be two hundred pounds, if not more, and the way it digs into the earth, clinging to the moss and wild grasses, it protests my thievery of its great heft.

As the sun reaches its zenith and the sweat drips off my face, heat baking into my skin, I finally feel something slip. Not my hands, but in my back. A long rubber band, elastic in its terror, unfurls up my spine as a scream escapes my lips. I collapse into the grass, rolling back and forth, trying to push my hands to my spine to rub the pain away. Stars in my black eyelids implode and turn to dust, the fragility of my simple skeleton revealing itself in throbbing wonder. I can't get up. I can hardly roll over on my back. And then I pass out.

$\sim$

Mosquitoes at my neck, stabbing, piercing, and I slap at my skin and moan into the darkness.

The darkness.

I try to sit up and a sharp pain shoots up my spine. I cut short the yelp that is pushing through my lips and open my eyes to the night. I have to get up—I have to get home. There's no reason I can think of that the wolves haven't found me yet.

I turn over onto my belly and push up with my hands until I'm on all fours. The irony is not lost on me. I bite into my lower lip as my face flushes red, filling my mouth with copper and heat and my vision dances in front of me. Tiny dots, I cannot see . . . wait, the dots are still moving.

A thin line of tiny yellow spheres extends over the grass, up the hill and ends at the front door to my hut.

Isabelle, my love.

"Thank you," I gasp.

And I start crawling. When the first howl shatters the dark, distorted and filled with echoes, down by the cliff's edge, I stop and consider the distance. The longer I sit here and think, the closer they get. And yet, I still can't move. I am submerged in an ocean of pain.

I lean back onto my knees and my eyes are coated with a thin film, a piercing hot rod running up my spine. I can barely breathe, a stuttering intake, but I know that I have to stand up. I place my hands on my knees and straighten out my back, and the darkness starts to shift at the horizon. I pull one leg forward and bracing my hands on my knee push myself into an upright position, standing tall, wobbling, starting to bend, to hunch over, wondering what it will feel like to walk.

I wonder what it will feel like to run.

I set one foot in front of me and find that if I focus on the trail of yellow lights, if I focus on my breathing, the traveling heat in the small of my back, now the middle of my back, now a knot of tension in my neck?

I can assign it to some other man—it is not my pain right now.

I walk as if I am a child. But there is no furniture nearby to balance me—padded and safe—sharp edges hidden from soft flesh. I am chubby legs wobbling, made of rubber, eager to bend at the slightest bit of resistance. I bark a laugh. This is how it will be—alpha to omega, womb to womb—all for a stupid piece of wood.

I don't dare look up, or down toward the cliff's edge, across the grass that sighs at my ineptitude. I take the steps I need to get to the door, I count the fireflies and inhale their buttery aroma, and I make it to the stone porch. I paw at the door, grabbing for the handle, sweat running down my neck, tears filling my eyes, and when I turn around to slam the door shut, ignoring the heat that is immolating my back, they swarm across the field and wrap around the house, disappearing into the night without a sound. I am still holding the door open wide—I am barely clinging to consciousness, my mouth filled with cotton and glass.

I close the door and the latch clicks shut. Numb, I ease to the bed, feeling my way in the darkness—and I lie down, glistening, sobbing. I lie down and close my eyes.

In the morning there is no pain.

This is how it goes.

I open the door to sunlight and the distant chirps of angry birds, stepping outside to see what fresh batch of horror awaits me. I walk to the back of the hut to the rain barrel, eager to drink the fresh water. Off into the distance is a long, black, shallow ditch that stretches out over the hill. At my feet sits the log. All up and down the rope are teeth marks buried in the frayed and tormented twine—and in my head, I hear her laughing.

LITTLE RED WAGON

REBECCA HATED HER father for what he'd done, refusing to help him dig the grave, arms crossed, tears running down her face, the body under the tarp no longer Grandpa, no more secret conversations when they were alone, just the two of them now—her father the killer, her father and his constant worries, her father convinced that the old man had finally fallen sick. They'd been alone for a long time now, the three of them living off the land, the radio antenna built up tall in the back yard, stretching up into the sky. Nobody ever answered, but she sat in the kitchen, turning the knobs, trying to find a sign of life, anyway. The black box sat on the table, static and interference crackling from the device, the puddle of blood on the floor where her grandfather had fallen, the hammer that killed him still lying there like a sleeping snake. Sitting next to her, the thick, black lab nuzzled her hand, whimpering. Sadie was upset, she didn't know what to do, and neither did Rebecca. She was a teenager now, but inside, she was still a child, a baby—and she felt helpless.

One percent, that's what Grandpa had said—only one percent had survived. This had been several years ago, when one percent meant something. He'd tug on his long, gray beard and stare at the television set as the man on the news rattled on, updates so infrequent, most of the population dead and gone now. Around them, the world had simply disappeared—no cars driving by, no planes overhead, with the farm still functioning, but just barely. Their pantry was filled with canned goods—it had been easy to drive around their small town and fill up the bed of their pickup truck with more. In the beginning the stench had been unbearable, meat going bad, bodies lying everywhere, but over time the animals and elements picked at the bones, leaving little behind but broken, white skeletons. One percent had turned into another one percent, and that's when it all went quiet, went dark. The second wave erupted, the mutation—airborne or dormant, nobody knew—and then no more frantic man on the television set, hair sticking out in all directions, shouting at the camera. No, there was nothing more after that.

Grandfather talked about keeping the race alive, that they had to find a female, a woman—that was why they had the radio going, why he'd built the tower, why they constantly scrolled up and down the dial, looking for any survivors. He was a handy man, Grandpa, able to build most anything out in the barn with his tools and charts—his years of engineering so helpful now that the world had moved on. A stack of books sat by his leather recliner—biomechanics, computer programming, artificial intelligence, and bionics.

"What's your earliest memory?" Grandpa asked her.

"What do you mean?"

"Think back," he said, easing into the recliner.

"What do you remember, the very first thing you can think of?"

Rebecca sat on the couch, and pulled her long, brown hair behind her head and into a ponytail, something she did when she was concentrating.

"Anything?" he nudged, his hands together in a steeple, pressed to his lips.

"I remember a little red wagon," Rebecca said, and he nodded. "And inside it are a bunch of puppies—little black bundles of fur. Was that here on the farm?" she asked.

Grandpa didn't answer, merely raised his eyebrows and grinned.

"They'd been born on the farm and I was taking them down to the end of the driveway, there were six of them, and we were going to give them away. You told me I could keep the last one, but only the last one. That must have been Sadie."

"What's two times two, Rebecca?"

"Four, silly."

"What's four times four?"

"16."

"12 times 12?"

"144."

Grandpa paused, looking at her, as Rebecca focused in on him, her eyes shifting, the pupils getting smaller, then larger, then smaller again.

"144 times 144?"

"20,736."

"Good girl," he said.

Rebecca stood in the kitchen, watching her father dig the grave, out beyond the apple trees, the shovel piercing the dirt, over and over again. She loved her grandfather, and didn't mind the private examinations. He said it was important, their little secret, and this is what her father had yelled at her about as he stood over her grandfather's body—but he was wrong, so very wrong. After the world went silent, after they'd filled the pantry with canned goods and planted a new harvest, made sure the pigs still had their slop, the chickens clucking at their feed—all they had was each other. The well wouldn't run dry, Grandpa assured them, they had water and food, and solar panels lining the roof, as well as the barn, the windmills spinning, always spinning, at the back of their twenty acres, down by the creek—Grandpa said he saw it coming, it was only a matter of time. He said a lot of things when she was lying on the cold metal table, out in the faded red barn.

In the beginning, she thought it was just part of her education. No school anymore, so Grandpa would toss out math questions, give her writing assignments, talk to her about history, and even human anatomy. It used to be exams at the kitchen table—stethoscope on her bony chest where breasts refused to grow—seemed she'd always been twelve years old. He'd look in her eyes and make noises, humming to himself, muttering okay and yes and just fine as he looked in her nose, checked out her sinuses, made her stick out her tongue.

He didn't start taking her out to the barn until her incident with the fingers. She came to him as he sat in the recliner, a book in his lap. Father was nowhere to be found. And if Rebecca had probed her memories, she'd find that to be very accurate—at first. She was pale as a sheet, sweat running down her face, the fingers on her right hand bent back and sideways at strange angles—no blood, merely broken bones, bent fingers.

"Grandpa?" she said, "Grandpa, help me, help me . . . something's wrong."

He leaped out of his seat, the book falling to the floor, Sadie sitting up, always the same weight, always black, her muzzle never getting gray, barking at the sudden movement and Rebecca's panicked voice.

"It's okay, sweetie," he said, rushing to her, as she stared down at her mangled hand, holding it gingerly but feeling no pain, sick to her stomach, and yet, no blood gushed forth. He put his hands on her shoulders.

"It's okay, I can fix it, I can splint it," he said.

She felt his hands on her neck, her shoulders, pressing down, as if searching for something, and then she fainted.

When she woke up her right hand was in a cast.

"It's okay, honey," her grandfather said. "It wasn't nearly as bad as you thought. A few fingers were merely jammed, two fractured, but I set them right. You should be okay. Any pain?" he asked.

Rebecca shook her head. There was no pain, none at all. She sat up on the cold metal table and looked around the barn. Sadie jumped up and placed her front paws on the steel table, licking Rebecca's bare leg.

And then, her father was around more. Suddenly he was a dominant presence on the farm—always keeping an eye on her, chopping wood, feeding the chickens, no longer the ghost or rumor that he used to be. Used to be, she'd think. She searched her memory for her father—she saw him driving away in a beige sedan, a salesman she thought, the letters popping up in her head like a neon sign. Then she saw him with a briefcase, walking in the front door. She saw him place airline tickets on the kitchen table and pour himself a cup of coffee. Yes, she saw her father well.

After the accident, she would meet Grandpa in the barn on a monthly basis, but only when her father was out cutting the grass or running the thresher. Her grandfather said it was because he had to run tests, diagnostics he called them, make sure everything was working right, and that it was okay for a doctor, for him now, but not in front of her father—he wouldn't understand. It always made her sleepy, lying on the table. He poked and prodded, mostly by her head, always studying her eyes, what he called optics, when he muttered to himself. He was gentle, always gentle, and by the time his hands were on her shoulders, her head, she'd fallen asleep.

The questions certainly didn't make Rebecca's father feel included, the way she and Grandpa would talk in the living room, math and science, complex equations and theorems, always going quiet when her father came into the room. They would laugh, and say that he had plenty of education already, go milk the cows, they'd chuckle, go toss some hay around, and they'd both make muscles, flex them, and her father would scowl, and leave the room. He never had a good sense of humor.

Her father was a quiet man, a big guy, strong and silent, a bit of a worker bee, she used to think to herself. Grandpa would say that he was so grateful her father was around more—now that he was getting old, and she could see it in his eyes, his hair and beard sprouting more white every day, the way his skin wrinkled, and the spots by his wrists. She worried about him. But it gave Rebecca comfort to see her father outside in the yard, splitting timber, lugging buckets of water or slop, bales of hay tossed around as if they were nothing, a downed tree cut, and cut and split, only the trunk left, a chain attached, a tractor pulling it, and then his massive arms wrapping around the roots, pulling it out and lifting it up, as if it were made of paper.

All it took was one time, one instance of her walking out of the barn buttoning up her blouse, and her father's scowl turned into rage. She heard them yelling, Grandpa assuring him it was science, there were no doctors now, he was the only mind they had, that he was just making sure Rebecca was healthy. Her father wasn't very trusting—almost simple at times. She'd seen him cry over a dead rabbit that had been gutted by a fox, holding the creature in his lap, rocking back and forth, so distraught. It had upset Rebecca—not the dead rabbit, it was just nature after all, but him, he had upset her, his reaction. No emotion, never laughing, never joking, never singing or dancing when Grandpa put on some music, but this—crying over the rabbit. It made no sense to her.

So she stood in the kitchen, and watched her father bury the old man, Sadie licking her hand. She was suddenly tired, her batteries run down, and so she went to her bedroom, and lay down on the floral sheets, staring out the window at the setting sun, orange turning to red, so tired, so sad. Maybe Grandpa had been sick after all, one percent of one percent of one percent.

She closed her eyes and replayed the scene at the

kitchen table, her Grandpa holding her hand, trying to explain something to her, what was out in the barn, frozen and kept for a reason. He spoke about her as if she were two entirely separate people—and he spoke of her father the same way. He talked about her mother, and when he said the word mother a jolt went through Rebecca, a wave of confusion crashing in her head—and where there should have been memories, nothing. He said he'd fix everything, in time. But he was getting old, he needed help, the work he'd done wouldn't last forever—the radio signal must be stronger. He spoke of amplifiers and how they might have to travel, all the while holding her hand, and yet, all she could do was stare at him—mother. It didn't add up, didn't compute. Why had she never asked about her mother, why was there nothing to cling to, no memory? Her father had walked in and stood by the door, his face an eternal frown.

The day after her grandfather had talked to her in earnest, trying to explain that they were running out of time, she lay in bed, not wanting to get up, a candle burning on her desk, vanilla and sandalwood drifting to the ceiling. Images of her mother came rushing back to her—hanging laundry on a clothesline outside, her auburn tresses flowing in the wind, her mother with an apron full of eggs, coming from the chicken coop, her mother singing a lullaby as she poured water over Rebecca's head in the bath, smiling as she did it.

"In time," her grandfather had said, standing in the doorway. "Give me time. I'll make it all whole again, I promise."

But now he was gone. Rebecca felt weak and unable to rise. On the floor by her bed, Sadie slept, hardly moving at all. Rebecca could feel the great shadow of her father in the doorway—standing there, silent.

"Dad?" Rebecca asked, tears in her eyes. "Dad, come here."

The big man lumbered over, Sadie not even raising her head.

"Tell me about my mother. I can hardly picture her. What happened, where did she go?"

He sighed and placed his hand over hers.

"I don't know, honey."

"What do you mean?" she said.

"I don't remember."

Rebecca stared at him, as she felt the energy draining out of her body.

"What do you remember?" she asked.

Her father sat there, arms heavy, his head hanging low, a soft whirring sound filling the air, his frame suddenly growing weak, the room dark and quiet.

"What's the first thing you remember? Go back as far as you can, what's your first memory?" Rebecca asked.

Her father stared at the floor, the gears turning, trying to think back, to remember, something from his childhood. He held her hand, no longer warm, cool to the touch.

"I remember a little red wagon," he said, and she nodded. "And inside it are a bunch of puppies—little black bundles of fur."

Rebecca closed her eyes, two tears slipping out, as her chest moved up and down, slowly, and then, not at all.

"They'd been born on the farm and I was taking

them down to the end of the driveway, there were six of them, and we were going to give them away. Somebody told me I could keep the last one, but only the last one. Who was that?" he asked the room. But there was no response—it remained silent.

He held his daughter's hand, now cold, the black lab at his feet not stirring, the house around him closing in, the silence deafening.

"What have I done?" he asked.

ASKING FOR FORGIVENESS

WE STAND AT the edge of the ancient forest, yellow blurry eyes weeping with sickness, as a cool breeze pushes through the leaves, the light flickering in the cabin, as the day starts to slip away. We are more than we were last month, double what was birthed last year, and none of us remember being upright—we stand on all fours now as if this was how we were made.

We watch the boy fill his bucket with sand, and then empty it, and then fill it again, sitting there with his short blonde hair and overalls, smacking his lips as we smack our warped mouths open and shut, not a care in the world, the lad, acres of dead land stretching out in every direction, her eyes on him from the kitchen, our eyes on him from the drifting shade.

Lips cracking as our fetid grins widen, the teeth come out—sour saliva spilling onto the dirt path, our gangly limbs shaking, sores mottled with flies and squirming maggots, waiting for the right time to claim him as our own.

The sun is descending, the moon slow to rise, and the boy still plays in the box, no sign of the change yet, a cough from him and he stands up slowly, thumb in his mouth, rubbing at his eyes with tiny fists, falling back down, and then gradually tipping over.

The screen door creaks open and she wipes her long, slender fingers on the stained, faded apron, a stray strand of yellow hair tucked back as she steps outside, slow to approach him, humming something under her breath, hoping the boy is tired, not shifting, hoping that the movement she sees in the encroaching woods is nothing more than the fluttering wind, her sigh in unison, the boy merely asleep.

We murmur mother, but her gaze only touches the edge of the yard, before darting away.

We must bide our time now, we were too early it seems, so we retreat to the cave, where one by one she brought us, hand in hand, down a long, winding path, thorny branches reaching out, nipping at our bare, mottled flesh. For each of us it was a secret, something she whispered to us in the middle of the night, her vanilla lavender lips on our foreheads, her promises and apologies falling on deaf, damaged ears. She was our mother, and we were her children. We trusted her when we were submerged in the bath—soap bubbles and laughter, pushing our heads under, but then lifting us back up. Her tears were tears of joy, we thought— she always brought us back up into the light, up out of the water. She never kept us under. Perhaps those hesitations, those extra seconds, went unnoticed.

On the nights when the moon filled the sky and the windows leaked light, she would open the creaking door and slip away for hours on end. What were we to think? She always had something to do—water from the well, fruit from the bent apple tree, down on her knees in the garden, pulling and grunting, basket over one arm, basket over the other, knife in the kitchen slicing, boiling water, oil heating, a slip here and there, a gasp and a red trickle, but these are the ways of the land. Nothing here was foreign.

The berries on the other side of the hill, sometimes strawberries, sometimes blue, her hair filled with twigs, the scratches up and down her arms most definitely from thorns, not him, the clothes drying on the line, her delicates, never dotted with blood, it must be the berries, we told ourselves. What did we know? We were babies, then—still babies now.

In the cave we snap at each other, and then huddle in the middle, pressed up against each other, for warmth, for companionship, out of habit, and memory, as we hope for something more. Perhaps tomorrow we will stop the cycle—or perhaps she will bring him here, the coward that she is.

Our father was a rumor, an echo, something only to be seen out of the corner of your eye. Our father was a woodsman, arms like tree limbs, beard as if born from bear, disappearing for days, for weeks, returning with so many things—tiny bird skulls, beads on a string, flowers for mother with purple blossoms and veiny leaves. The wood was stacked along one side of the cabin as high as it could go, the steady chop, the split of the timber, just part of the day, or so we were told. Our father was the cold creek that ran south of our home, filled with silver-backed fish with blood-orange meat, whispering every time we neared it, quenching our thirst, promises of sleepy peace if only we'd step a bit closer. Our father was the frosty moon that pasted the land with silence as our breath formed clouds of pain, feet bruised and bleeding, his laughter running over the mountain, guiding us down one ravine and up the other, wandering from hill to valley and back, some elusive destination always out of reach. Our father was time, stretched in every direction, elastic as a rubber band, as slow and anchored as a wall of granite, our eyes closing, waking up sore, grey where black had been. All lies. Everything she had ever told us was a lie. She never loved us, or it wouldn't be like this.

In the night there is a flash of silver, our father returned, and in the morning, I stand alone at the edge of the woods. I heard them crying, I saw him approach, his hand on each one of us, muttering kind words, his voice nearly forgotten, his muscled grip soothing, then choking, then ripping, the piercing of flesh, and my kin was held down, one by one, eyes wide open, and yet, disbelieving. I too, did not move, did not understand. Perhaps she had seen us, feared us, known what we planned to do, the bloodline destined to end by our teeth and claws and squinting eyes. Father would not allow it, he had returned with thunder and lightning and vengeance—a great rain pouring down outside, washing away our sins. I alone was spared, the eldest.

Alone now, I've lost my way, finding it hard to leave the cave, until the stench grows so foul that I force myself to grab them, one by one, and drag their filthy bodies down the rocky path that spilled to the east, casting them over the edge of the mossy cliff, one by one, not looking down, not taking note, merely laboring on because questions still remained.

Why me?

Why any?

ASKING FOR FORGIVENESS

With nothing left to do but watch and wait, I would wake when the sun pushed into the cave, and stumble down to the edge of the forest, smoke rising out of the stack, the woodpile never shrinking, something he could do right, and I would stare at her as she opened the creaking door, bucket of water tossed outside, a sigh and her hands on her back, bending backward and moaning, taking a deep breath, swelling up again, the moon reaping its harvest. I wanted to hate her, as much as I wanted her praise—anything, any gesture at all, so hungry I was for even a scrap. Back inside and then out with a basket, laundry on the line, the boy stepping gingerly behind her, walking now, his head on a swivel, this way and that, sniffing the air, his hand reaching out for her hem, taller now, a twitch in his shoulders, scanning the land for what, I do not know.

When she finally brings me the boy, I can see he is not well, this experiment she keeps trying, once again a disaster. He is naked, standing, but beginning to hunch over, his eyes a cream like spoiled milk, his lips distended, teeth pushing around his mouth in crooked horror, his hand in hers, as she stands there, swelling, tears in her eyes, rubbing her mouth with the back of her hand, speaking my name. I had forgotten my name.

Her hand is on my neck, rubbing, patting, petting, as she pleads with me to take care of him, to not grow bitter, to find it in my heart to welcome my brother into the woods, while she tries once again to find a cure. I do not hate her any longer, my mother, my beacon, for the land is empty. My father continues his long walks in every direction—north into the cold, the winter and frost, fingers ruddy and numb; south into the dry heat, vultures, tumbleweeds and one false oasis after another.

She will continue to try, in this barren wasteland to be the mother that no one else can be. She will not let us expire, this last great race, she will not let it all end with a whimper and a cough, a last gasp and shuddering sickness, she will swim in the water, she will kneel in the moonlight, she will pray to the lost gods, and bleed in her solitude, my father standing with his shadow cast out, darkness ever creeping, asking for forgiveness.

BALANCE SHEET

THE DAY THEY came for my daughter was an ordinary day, the fields of soybeans full of lush greenery, the harvest soon to come, my retirement in full swing, Talia standing before me, angry with a red face, two men in gray jumpsuits trying to hold her still. She'd been like this for a few years now, her mother gone, possibly dead, always absent anyway, the birth never taking, the baby a shrieking alarm in her ears, until one day, she simply walked away. Unfathomable was the word I often muttered to myself, and it rattled around my skull today as I sat in my kitchen, a tiny house at the edge of the farm, a humble existence, the crop all mapped out, the plans set in motion, my years as an accountant come to an end. Talia stood tall, with her head shaved in defiance, her long black hair a distant memory, tied with a piece of string, and hidden in a drawer. But I loved my daughter, and would do anything for her, so of course I said yes—I would protect her today—that was my job, as her father, wasn't it? And as a former CPA I have to admit that I checked off a little box in my head, this immediate idea of justice appealing to me in some way, balancing things out, accounts payable, accounts receivable. She was still a child, barely out of high school, still wandering in the world, looking for something. So, of course I said yes.

He wasn't anything special, really, the man in the black suit, picking at his teeth with his long fingernails. I offered him coffee as I sat at the kitchen table, my mug steaming—the smell of bacon filling the air. He was a gangly man, with empty black eyes, his pale wrists sticking out a bit beyond the dingy white dress shirt, the black cuffs rubbed raw at the edges.

"You understand how this works, Mr. Jones? It's her first offense, but the cameras don't lie."

He pointed to the laptop sitting open on the scarred, wooden table, my daughter snatching some candy bars, dropping them in her jacket pocket, eyes darting this way and that. I hardly recognized her.

"Yes, I understand."

"So you choose the second option, Mr. Jones. No trial, immediate justice right here, right now. I'm a busy man, you see, lots of stops to make. Your daughter, Talia is it, yes, Talia," he says, leaning over the computer, tapping a few keys, "three days shy of her eighteenth birthday, so technically she's still a minor."

I nod my head.

"That's a good thing, Mr. Jones."

I will come to think of him as a phantom, Agent Allen. He will haunt my dreams, my waking life. I will see his square, yellow teeth, his bookish glasses, his long fingers, everywhere I go.

"I understand all of this, agent. I will take door number two, yes. We can take care of this right now, I understand that she is my responsibility."

I take a sip of coffee as his smile widens.

BALANCE SHEET

"Dad, no, don't," Talia says. "You don't have to do this. Honest. It was a simple mistake, it won't happen again."

I look at my daughter, my little angel, my flower, and while I hear her voice, I do not seriously consider letting her go downtown, no matter how quickly Agent Allen says she would be tried. She will not sit in a cell, brooding, exacting revenge on anyone but herself, the circumstances that put her there, the people that contributed to her acting out. No, I will up the ante right now and show her there are others that suffer when she breaks the law, starting with her father.

"What do I need to sign, Agent Allen?" I ask.

Talia starts to cry, no longer struggling, it has been decided.

"Here we go," he says, whipping out a few sheets of folded paper from his jacket pocket. I sign here and here and initial there, and it's done.

"Thank you, Mr. Jones. You are a fine, upstanding citizen. Now, if you could place your hand on the table, please."

Talia doesn't speak, her head hung, pale skin taking on a green tint, the men holding her up, silent, their faces void of emotion.

I place my hand on the table, my left hand of course, and Agent Allen leans down and picks up his black, leather briefcase off the floor, placing it on the table, clicking it open, depositing the paperwork, and taking out a slim metal device that looks something like an electric toothbrush.

"There will be pain, of course," he says, "but not a lot of blood."

I nod my head.

"You ready?" he asks.

"Yes, go ahead."

"Good thing she's seventeen, that's all I have to say, Mr. Jones," and he cuts off the tip of my left index finger. The laser held between two thin, metal posts at the end of the device is quick and efficient, one squirt of blood, cauterizing as it cuts through the flesh and bone. I open my mouth to scream, and then it's done. The tip sits there as if looking for a lost brother, a space between it and the rest of my hand. It is an illusion, a parlor trick. The agent puts his toy away, and reaching down with a disinfectant wipe, makes sure the finger is sealed, cleaning up the streak of blood on the table.

The men let go of Talia, and the agent tosses the tip to her.

"Here you go, sweetheart."

She opens her mouth, aghast, the tip bouncing around in her hands, leaving little red blotches every time it touches her, falling to the floor.

"No offense, Mr. Jones," he says, "but I hope I don't see you again. Have a nice day, you two."

Talia is at my side, she is crying, apologizing, and I sit like stone, feeling that I've made the right choice, but sick to my stomach nonetheless. She is my daughter, and I love her and it was a small sacrifice. But I wanted her to learn something here, to see how her actions ripple out into the world like a stone in a pond.

"You have a birthday coming up," I whisper, as she kneels next to me, crying. "Let's do something fun, okay?"

And things are just fine for a bit. But kids will be kids, and the crowd she started running with, they

Balance Sheet

wanted to make a difference, they wanted to change the world. The next time I saw Agent Allen was a few years later, standing in my kitchen again, his goons holding my daughter, accusing her of spying, treason, grand larceny—explaining to me the options here, my choices, as I nodded my head, and sipped my coffee. Talia stood tall, defiant, an entirely different creature than the first time. She was my daughter, and I loved her, and it was my job to protect her, even from herself. She was nineteen now, and could stand trial for her actions, or, as the law stated, any family member could voluntarily help them administer immediate justice, right here and now. No court, no trial, no crowded jail cell—simply the videos playing out before me, Agent Allen standing there with his toy, its jaw widened now, not for a finger, but for the entire hand. And a second device, a long, metal stick with a buzzing device at the end, spinning and crackling with electricity. But I can hardly hear his voice, my eyes on Talia, angry again, always so angry, tears running down her face, her pleas landing on deaf ears. She would learn this time, I would make sure of it. There were four men in gray jumpsuits today, two to hold her, and two to hold me. The hand, and then the eyes, it seems. Lasers separating flesh from bone, taking my sight as the room fills with the smell of burning flesh, her screams mingling with mine, and then it all goes dark.

I love my daughter. It's my job to protect her.

∽

I can hear her singing over by the stove, Talia, as I sit

-157-

at the table. It is a new table, white Formica, something she tells me she found in a thrift store, with gray swirls and shiny metal framing the edges, which I can feel with my right hand—my fingers. She tells me the chairs are yellow vinyl on the backs, and a white cream for the seats. I have to take her word for it. She is making chicken noodle soup, it's cold outside, the crop taken in, snow on the ground, and she's telling me about a man she met at the university. Her hair has grown back out, it's long now, and I imagine she looks a lot like her mother.

"Is he a student?"

"No, a teacher. Philosophy," she says.

I pause and wonder—this man full of ideas.

I hear the grilled cheese sandwich sizzling in the pan. She doesn't get out here to the farm that often now—busy taking classes in the city, still trying to figure out who she is, and that's okay. I understand. And I don't want to be trouble, ask her for too much. She has already shoveled the walk, taken the garbage cans down to the end of the driveway, tidied up around the house. I can take care of myself, I've memorized the layout, it wasn't that hard, only a handful of rooms, but I want her to feel needed. Because she is needed, I love my daughter—her visit is the highlight of my day, my week—my month. I love her with all of my heart.

I feel her hand on my shoulder and a kiss on my cheek, the soup and sandwich in front of me, and she joins me for the meal, and we catch up. She tells me about this man, and I worry of course, I'm her father after all. But she sounds happy, she tells me about her classes, some bands she saw recently, and I nod my head and listen, chime in when I can, but for the most part I eat my soup, and every once in a while I feel her hand on my arm, and I smile. I picture her face as I remember it, as a child, smiling up at me, holding my hand at the playground, laughing on the swings—scrambling up and down the slides. It's how I see her now, my eyesight gone, always as a child. And I'm not sure why.

When she has left, I stand at the sink and do the dishes—I wouldn't let her clean up, I have to show her I can take care of myself, I don't want her to feel bad, to worry. We don't talk about the men in gray jumpsuits, about Agent Allen. We pretend it never happened, the elephant in the room at all times.

I retire to the small living room off the kitchen and turn on the television set, slipping into the leather recliner. I reach for the remote with my left hand, my coffee cup in my right, an old habit, and I laugh. I still feel it sometimes, the phantom hand, and when I say that word in my head, phantom, I see the face of Agent Allen, and I frown. I hold no animosity for him, just doing his job, but I break out in a slight sweat anyway. I think of Talia driving into the city by herself, and I hope this man is a good man, somebody at the other end of the line that will be nice to her, support her, and see how special she is, my daughter. Placing my cup down, I grab the remote with my right hand now, chuckling to myself, clicking the television on. I set the remote down on the end table, and then touch my right cheek where she kissed me goodbye—a whiff of her perfume floats to me, sandalwood and red currant, and a hint of something darker.

∽

"Adultery," is what Agent Allen says, standing in my kitchen again. They've taken her outside, her screams were drowning out the agent, we couldn't talk, two more men in gray jumpsuits, and I wonder if they're the same. I have no way of knowing. I guess the man at the university . . . I guess he wasn't so nice after all. Wife and two kids, so achingly predictable, and I'm disappointed in Talia. I cannot see her face, but I can hear her pleading with me from the yard, her explanations, she is in love, he is going to leave his wife. I don't ask what will become of him, because I don't really care. He is a distant shadow filled with black hair and slick flesh and hidden lust and my head is throbbing with a swarm of bees.

"All parties will be dealt with, Mr. Jones," he continues, "I don't make the laws, they continue to evolve, I understand your questions, certainly I do, and she's a woman now, sir, if you don't mind my saying so . . ."

And he goes on and on. I am cold. They've taken my clothes off, preparing for the inevitable, I suppose. They know me by now, my motivations, how I work, I expect. I run my trembling fingers over my skin, dry and winkled in places, sagging stomach, aching back, but the men with their hands on my shoulders, they are not there to keep me, as if I could run, they are merely there to hold me up, I suspect.

I love my daughter.

WHITE PICKET FENCES

I'D BEEN PAINTING Mrs. Johnson's fence all week, the sun beating down on me hot as hell, a jar of sun tea brewing on her front porch, lemons cut up and floating in a big glass jar, one rumbling Chevy after another cruising up and down the strip, but all I could think about was Connie, and the smell that was coming from the basement. It was a strange mix, the sweat and exhaustion washing over me, the call of the movie house, the plaid skirts, the poodle skirts, jeans rolled up to show some ankle, one girl after another walking those black and white saddle shoes up and down the concrete, their cat-eye glasses peeking at me, my t-shirt soaked through. But, Connie—I could watch her suck the pop out of a soda for the rest of my life, for sure. And lurking underneath this all, every time I went around back for a new gallon of paint, was the thick stench of something dead from the cellar doors, the heavy padlock, the paint flecked and peeling, the grass worn away to reveal a dirt path that ran all the way around to the sidewalk.

I like Mrs. Johnson enough, she paid pretty well, and I couldn't beat the location. Just catty-corner was the Sonic, where all the kids were hanging out, and even though I was hard at work, I got a glimpse of the girls in my class, a bit of shiny metal or maybe a flash of red paint, just enough to make me feel like I was there, just enough to make me work harder, to try and finish this job. She'd come out to check on me, as I worked on the fence that ran all around the perimeter of her property, a cigarette in one hand, her sunglasses on, and some sort of housecoat, as if she were an old maid, but I knew what she hid underneath that long, floating outfit. I'd seen her in the back yard in her bikini, slathered in baby oil, glistening like a seal, her lips a dark red that just begged to be on my neck. The heat was getting to me, Connie and Mrs. J, her wink and a nod, a glass of that tea, it was fine with me, I guess. What else was I gonna do this summer, sit down by that greasy lake and smoke cigarettes, starting rumors about girls that none of us had kissed? It was torture, and yet, I had nowhere else to go.

"Jimmy, you getting thirsty?" Mrs. Johnson asked, standing on the front porch. I was definitely getting thirsty, I was damn tired, and it was hardly noon, my nights filled with the smell of dead cats and shadows moving in and out of the bushes, my dreams filled with her house, the yard, the cellar doors, when I should have been thinking about Connie.

"Sure, Mrs. Johnson," I said, putting down the brush and walking over.

"Jimmy, how many times have I told you to call me Grace? You're making me feel ancient, hon."

"Sure thing, Mrs. Johnson. I mean, Grace," I said, sucking down the iced tea, as she patted me on the shoulder, a floral scent filling my nostrils, jasmine or something, cedar and bourbon underneath.

"How's it going? You gonna finish up this week you think? I'll bet the lake is calling, right? And how about that Connie?"

"What about her?" I asked, turning to face her.

"Oh, I see her walk by here all the time, honey. I'm not dense. I mean, how many burgers can that girl eat? I've never seen her take a bite. I think that's the same Walgreens bag she's been carrying around all summer, I haven't seen her lipstick color change even once," she laughed.

"Oh. Her. I don't know, Mrs. Johnson . . . Grace. I mean, she's cute and all. I better get back to painting."

I never paid that much attention to how many times Connie came and went. I mean, it seemed like she was always there, but how many times was I imagining it, wishing her onto the street, her eyes glancing over, that little wave, her blonde hair pulled back into a ponytail?

I went around to the back to get some more paint, the cellar doors rattling, but me only wishing for a breeze. I eyed the padlock, as the shadows in the basement window swam and unfurled, my eyes rolling back up into my head, the grass rushing up to me in one fell swoop.

∽

Opening my eyes, I could feel the cool air around me, the room dark and musty, shelves on one side filled with jars of canned pickles and peppers, tomatoes and green beans. And on the far wall, a workbench, covered in dust, a rusty saw lying out, a bag of lye, a bag of soil, some rock salt, and that smell washing over me, causing me to gag.

"Here, drink some water," she said, stepping out of the shadows, handing me a glass.

I was lying on a cot, an old army canvas thing, down in her basement, Grace standing with one hand on her hip, the other holding that damn cigarette, exhaling smoke as if it were a chore.

"You passed out, sonny boy, heat got to you, I guess. I told you to take it easy."

"That smell . . . "

"I know, it's horrible, I'm sorry, something died down here and for the life of me, I can't track it down. A squirrel, a possum, something got in here and never got out," she laughed, her eyes glancing over to the bench, to the corner where a huge steamer trunk sat, a stain around it, seeping into the concrete. Her lipstick was smeared to one side, her house coat popping a few buttons on the bottom, a lot of leg showing, her eyes dancing as she inhaled.

"You okay, Grace?"

She smiled, and exhaled smoke, laughing. "Yeah, I just don't like being down here. I couldn't think of another way to cool you off; I was worried you were sick or hurt."

"You carried me down here?"

She eyeballed me. "You don't remember walking? You really are out of it," she said. "Why don't you take the rest of the day off, you're making good progress. We can pick this up tomorrow."

I stood up, a bit dizzy, but okay.

"I should probably clean up a bit down here anyway," she moaned, and her lip trembled, her gaze easing over to the shadows again, a tear pushing its way out of her left eye, turning away from me."

"You okay, Grace?"

"Oh, honey," she said, staring into the shadows. "I'm just fine," she said, the clammy basement pushing goose bumps over my skin. Outside a car horn honked, and I looked over at the steps leading out and up, the flash of sunlight filling the opening, and it seemed like a million miles away. "There's nothing you could do anyway," she muttered.

"What's that?" I asked, taking a step toward her.

"Go on, get," she said, waving me away. "You can't fix everything around here, Jimmy, I have to be more independent, you know, do these things myself. Can't rely on a man to help me out every time I stub my toe, break something, or have to bury some dead thing or another."

I stared at her for a moment, a long red scratch running around the back of her neck, her back to me as she inhaled on that cigarette, leaning into the shadows, and that trunk.

"Grace?"

"Go on, Jimmy. I'll see you tomorrow, but not too early, sleep in a bit, get some rest."

I took a step toward the cellar door, as she took a step toward that trunk, and outside I heard a car backfire, up the steps, the light and heat blanketing me, and then I was outside, back into the oven, leaving her behind, the paint cans lined up by the back door, the brush already washed off, and then it was down the sidewalk, heading home. I tried to clear my head, wondering what I might say to Connie the next day, what she might like to hear, a station wagon drifting by, kids in the back licking at their ice cream cones, the mother up front, her hair in curlers, her hands tapping on the steering wheel, the music up loud so she could sing along, something about a hotel, something about heartbreak, the guitar riffing and in the distance a scream, or maybe it was nothing, turning my head back toward the house, walking on, tired of it all. Connie was at the edge of my hazy vision, her tapping pencil in math class, her white teeth biting into a crimson apple at lunch, the way she scrunched up her nose when taking a test. She was an oasis in a desert, but I couldn't find my way to her.

∞

The note on the kitchen table said to water the flowers out front, and so that's what I was doing. Dad was off to work, mother to a PTA meeting or a book club, and I stood in front of the house watering the azaleas, the hanging plants, staring outward as if consulting a crystal ball. And then she was standing there, at the end of the sidewalk, Connie, with a clipboard in her hand, smiling.

"Hey, Connie," I said, leaning over to turn off the hose. "What are you doing in this neck of the woods?"

"Hi," she said. "Are you having a good summer, Jimmy? Still working on Mrs. Johnson's house?"

I soaked her up, every inch of exposed flesh, her tan arms, her long legs—the bit of color at her neck, her sun-kissed cheeks. She was like a page out of a Sears catalog, everything crisp and clean, buttoned up, tied back, her eyes like two sparkling jewels.

"Yeah," I said. "It's been hot, took a little time off yesterday. You? What's with the clipboard?"

"Oh, this," she said. "Pork and Corn Roast, down at First Methodist? You ever go?"

"Oh sure, lots of fun," I said, pushing my hands into my pockets, trying to stop my smile from expanding and eating my entire face.

"Well, we could use some help, you have any time at night maybe? I'm volunteering, but the men need help with the pigs—they're just huge, I tell you. I don't know how they do it. They sent me out to find some extra muscle to help out. What do you think, you qualify?"

"That sounds swell, Connie. I should ask my parents, but I think it'd be just fine. If Mrs. Johnson doesn't kill me first," I laughed.

She took a few steps forward with the clipboard in her hand.

"Here are the dates, maybe just put your name down for a few of the slots? I'm doing Friday and Saturday for sure," she grinned.

I took the board from her, the pencil too, looking down, working hard to keep my eyes off of her for a moment, as she stood next to me now, and I tried to remember my name, and how to spell it, a lawnmower starting up down the street, and she pressed in closer, our shoulders touching, baby powder and vanilla, my head starting to swim, as she pointed to a few lines, here and there. I wrote my name down, and looked up.

"Thanks, Connie. I guess I'll see you there, then."

She took the board from me and turned to walk away.

"It's a date!"

And then she eased on down the sidewalk, my eyes glued to her every movement, my throat dry—a swallow and I'm breathing again, and then she turns the corner on down the street, smiling and waving, and I wave right back.

∾

It's another hour before I finally get over to Mrs. Johnson's house, and it's quiet, not a person in sight, too early for the burger joint, the front door closed, but no answer to my knock. I head around back and the cellar door is wide open, and scattered around the back yard are holes—one, two, three of them, more even, maybe ten. The smell is even worse than the day before, and I lean over the nearest hole and see nothing but pairs of black patent leather shoes. In the next one there are belts and watches, the metal flashing up at me, the leather like a nest of snakes.

"What the hell?" I ask. "Mrs. Johnson? Grace?" I say and head toward the cellar. On the ground is a clipboard—a pencil snapped in two, and a trail of slimy liquid leading down into the basement.

"No, no, no . . . " I mutter.

The stench gets worse as I ease down the steps, something pungent and fishy, the slime stretching out across the concrete all the way to the open steamer chest, Mrs. Johnson with her back to me, her housecoat wide open, doing something with her hands, her arms moving, a smacking sound like chewing gum, or eating a plate of ribs. On the floor around her is water, everywhere, up to her ankles pushing toward me, flowing out of the trunk. Her hands come down to her sides, blood up to her elbows, her back still to me, the saw on the workbench wet with crimson, a hammer glistening in red, and there is motion in the trunk, something stirring in the shadows, the skin of a snake, a tentacle perhaps, a slick surface of some kind curling and expanding, and then she turns, her face full of eyes, dozens of them, blinking, staring, her hair floating wide and electric, bare breasts hanging down, her legs parting as she births onto the floor one tiny creature after another, slimy little heads, translucent skin, slipping down her legs and onto the floor, her mouth a beak now, clicking open and shut.

"Jimmy, I'm glad you're here."

And she takes a gliding step toward me, the water rising, green-scaled feelers pushing out of the trunk, her eyes swirling as the birthing continues, darkness pushing in from every corner of the room, and I am stone, I have lost my voice, a buzzing in my ears.

"It turns out I really do need your help," she says.

And the tentacles wrap around me, the babies scuttling up my legs, nipping as they go, her hands on my shoulders pushing the clacking beak to my neck and it is not the kiss I had thought about—her plump red lips on mine, wet tongue in my mouth—her beak instead tearing into my flesh, too weak and giving. I think of Connie, and what happened this morning, how clean and pure she smelled, the gleam in her eyes—I focus on that instead, thinking of how that night might have gone, holding her hand as we strolled around the church grounds, knowing now there is no God, but pushing that away for a moment, smiling as I pretend that maybe something else could have happened instead of this.

CHASING GHOSTS

THIS WIND OUTSIDE our apartment isn't a woman screaming, but there are nights I wake up in a panic, struggling to catch my breath. The garbage disposal becomes a rabid dog, its teeth nipping at my fingertips. The slam of the front door turns our apartment into a tomb sealed shut as my wife disappears out into the night, leaving me for dead. I can't trust myself to recognize the truth. Her lips on mine taste bitter, so I build a fortress around myself out of the evidence that is gathering. I wait to confront her, anxious for it to spill out into the daylight for everyone to see. I need to prove I am right.

My mind is telescoping away from me, all the way to my office, but Candace is naked under the warm blankets and my stomach twists in knots. The drapes are drawn, the room still dim, the white down comforter piled like drifts of snow. She's not trying very hard, with those doe-eyes of hers, not saying a word to convince me, and that's all it would take, one word: *Stay*. But I'm late for work.

"David, could you get me some lotion?"

"Sure." I grab the bottle off the dresser and hold it out to her.

"My back," she says. "Would you rub some on my back?"

She sits up on the edge of the wrought-iron bed, facing away from me, the sheet slipping down. The curve of her hips is hypnotizing. I kneel on the bed and squirt lotion onto my hands and rub it into her shoulders, down her spine, each tiny bump like a step up a staircase to some higher state of enlightenment. It isn't that I don't want to stay—I never want to leave. That's her power, her way of making me weak. It's like this every day. But if I exhaust her, maybe she won't stray.

When she turns around, her green eyes come up to meet mine, and her hands run up the front of my pants, squeezing. I close my eyes. Her mouth is at my neck, her tongue sliding between my lips. It looks like I'm going to be late. She pulls at my shirt, buttons popping, grabbing at my zipper, and she blankets me, pushing me down, climbing on top as she pushes me inside her. Hands on my shoulders, her eyes closed, her long black hair sways back and forth. As the tempo increases and my body glistens under a sheen of sweat, she cups her breasts, tugging at her nipples. That's something new—and I shudder.

$\backsim$

Keeping her happy isn't cheap and it costs me something every day. There is a long ride ahead of me—a bus to a subway into the city, and a METRA train out to a forlorn office at the edge of an industrial park. Down in the kitchen I suck down a tall glass of water, the white cabinets a snowstorm around me. I pull on a long, black wool coat over a cable-knit sweater and a turtleneck while the wind beats against the frozen panes of glass. I lace up my boots, her perfume still on my hands. Sliding on the black leather gloves, my eyes glance up to the ceiling, everything quiet above me. I have to go while the siren sleeps.

It's two blocks to the end of the street, the corner of Milwaukee and Wolcott, and Candace floats along with me. Her body, her pale skin, it's as if she's right here with me—a ghost. My breath drifts out in transparent clouds and when I inhale my lungs turn to ice. My paycheck, the overtime—this is what propels me out into the cold. I turn away from her so we can get ahead, save for a house in the suburbs, children and a life together—the American dream. These are lies I tell myself; they hold no weight; it's a façade and we both know it. I do it to keep her on a long leash. Candace is beyond my control. She has nothing but time and she likes to play with me, tease me, pull my strings and watch me dance. She is a Cheshire grin leaking out of the darkness.

Picking up the pace, I start to jog, because I can't miss this bus. From around the corner gears shift, the wide load of metal easing down Milwaukee toward me, the brakes squealing out in resistance. It's twelve blocks south to my el train, further and further away from my wife. This is one of many connections I'll have to make. My train is on its way into the city, coming all the way from Elgin, a huddled mass of rotting buildings at the edge of the Chicago River. It isn't into the station just yet, but it will be soon. It won't wait for me, and neither will my wife of six months. Candace used to get itchy—her eyes would wander, but I think she only strayed the one time. I see it in her face when she won't hold my gaze. It wasn't there today, not yet anyway, but maybe tomorrow or the next day. I'm helpless to do anything about it. There's a credit card sitting on the kitchen table, our tiny duplex of an apartment filled with cinnamon and musk. Half a pot of coffee waits for her and I hope she takes the money. I pray that she only spends my money today.

Another day has slipped away, and my gut says she's still being faithful. Part of my morning ritual is searching for clues as I'm getting ready for work. Sucking down coffee and trying not to sweat I keep one eye on her shadow, the other wide open for anything suspicious as I dart from room to room. I'm searching for receipts, for cash, for clothing sitting in the washing machine—I sniff her blouse, her jeans, her panties. In the shower drain there is a wad of hair stuck inside the trap. Pulling it out, I hold the knot up to a row of light bulbs over the sink—and scrutinize it. The only option for hair color here is brown, and my reflection in the mirror is of a pale man lost and frantic. I count the condoms in my dresser drawer buried under faded white tube socks and outdated argyle patterns. These are condoms she doesn't even know about but I check them anyway. I make sure they are the exact same ones, staring at the expiration dates, wondering who will last longer—them or us. I scour the phone bill for unknown numbers and some of them I call. They turn out to be Macy's, the library, a firing range out in Lake Zurich that's closed at the moment, the Walgreens pharmacy and her gynecologist. They're all suspicious, all part of some master plan, some complicated puzzle and I can't see the whole picture. We don't own a gun; she doesn't like Macy's; and I've never seen her read a book. The accusations have to wait until that night, another long day of stomach cramps, gobbling down aspirin, waiting for her to reappear.

"Where have you been, Candace? It's almost midnight."

She stands at the bottom of the steps, staring up at me. In the dark I can't see if she's smiling. Her face is still in the shadows.

"Just running errands, David. My cell phone battery died. Stupid stuff—returning a pair of jeans that were too expensive, I know how much you worry about money. I took your book to the library. It was almost due, so I extended it—you have three more weeks."

"Oh."

"You're not going to ask me about the gun?" Candace asks.

"What gun?" I say.

"The Firing Range. What about that?" She stays in the shadows.

"You planning on killing me?" I ask.

"It's a bar and grill, baby—The Firing Range? Organic, free range chicken . . . you know, I told you about dinner with my friend Melissa."

"Melissa, the brunette, works at Macy's—right."

"You know I don't like guns," she says.

"Well, I'm just glad you're okay."

Candace talks in her sleep. Sometimes it's simple words, a chain of *nononono* in a hushed breath. This isn't as bad as the *yesyesyes* uttered in the same husky moan. I hear names sometimes but they're safe names, those of her brother, her father, a friend of ours, my own name, but said in ways that don't seem familiar. *I'll meet you at the Bongo Room. I'll meet you at Feast*, she says. Is she speaking to me?

Those were our haunts, places we used to sit and eat in silence. We spooned up the chilled gazpacho with minced cucumber and chives in the relentless summers filled with heat and bare flesh. We chewed grilled skirt steak with garlic roasted mashed potatoes in the crippling winters, oblivious to the world under our layers of blankets. We stared at each other and I told her she was stunning, I told her she was my world. She nodded, swallowed the arugula, and ordered more red wine.

Candace is making me a lunch. She hasn't done that in months. The cutting board is littered with breadcrumbs, thin slices of cucumber peel, and a large bag of whole grain chips. I slip into my boots and pull on my long wool coat.

"I wanted you to have a healthy lunch, for once," she says, her back to me as she chops away, fuzzy pink robe pulled tightly around her figure, her calf muscles and bare feet a distraction. "And it saves us a bit of money too."

Somebody has stolen my tainted bride and replaced her with Martha Stewart.

"I'm almost done, just a bit of the Dijon mustard you like. Here's your coffee—cream and three sugars."

She turns around for a second to hand me the coffee, her hair in a ponytail, looking young and fit. I take a sip while she finishes up the lunch. It's perfect.

CHASING GHOSTS

"There's a treat in the bottom of the bag. You might want to eat alone," she says, standing on her toes to give me a kiss. "Just so you don't forget me."

"How could I ever do that?" I say.

"You better go, you'll be late," she says, pushing me toward the front door.

On any given day I take a bus to a train to a job. Sitting in a room above a storefront, my eyes constantly wander to the windows, trying to see the Chicago skyline, working at a computer, designing graphics all day long. I edit advertisements, create logos, and Candace is in every pixel of my work. My color palettes are pulled from her body: Pantone 201, her pouting red lips; Pantone 348, her jealous eyes; Pantone 607, her vanilla skin. Searching through stock photo sites for images of women, they all turn out looking like her. Every ad for Red Lobster, every newspaper insert for Libertyville Toyota, every billboard for Tylenol has a semblance of my wife. Her doppelganger is holding up shrimp; she is sitting behind the wheel, winking; she is faking a headache.

Lunch has lost its appeal so I toss the bag in the garbage can under my desk. Then I remember my treat. I fish the bag back out and look inside, a photo lurking at the bottom of the brown paper sack, bent but unmistakably capturing her naked body reclined on our bed. I want to believe that she took it herself. My anxiety leads me to wander down the streets of Elgin searching for answers in every brick wall and rusted pipe. It wasn't always like this.

She phones me several times a day, my caller ID a Pavlovian response, my forehead immediately moist.

I miss you, she says. *How is your day going?* I chew on my tongue and stare at the display.

"Who is M Dempsey?" I ask.

"What? Melissa, remember? My friend from college, the brunette?"

"Oh."

"I have to go, honey, I just wanted to make sure you were okay."

She hangs up but not before she giggles into the phone. The last word she mumbles is idiot, I think. Or maybe I'm hearing things—so far away from her. I'm in China chewing on bamboo shoots as I wander through the rice paddies. Or walking on the red, cratered surface of Mars, dust and rocks on a horizon I can never reach. I call the number back. It rings and rings, no voice mail picking up, no answering machine—nothing. Who does that? Who has no way of leaving a message in this day and age? Nobody. A cover does, a false identity. The rest of my day is spent hitting redial. I import an image for the ad I'm working on, trying to put the pieces together, and it's larger than the sum of its parts—a handful of tea leaves in the bottom of a china cup, trying to tell me something. As I work on a logo for the new Ford Fusion, her image appears—long legs wrapped around some shadow of a man, the opposite of whatever I am. At three fifteen I walk slowly into the bathroom and vomit into the toilet in stall number two. There is nothing but coffee and regret.

The ride home is in reverse. Taking the Elgin METRA train into the city, brick apartment buildings flying by, every dirty window is filled with her silhouette. I stand numb drifting up the escalator and out into the masses, short skirts and wide shoulders littering the sidewalks. I walk past the Sears Tower, its shadow a blanket of cold. In one hundred steps the entrance appears, jutting out of the fractured concrete, the Blue Line el back to Wicker Park where my bus never appears—another part of the conspiracy. My legs keep moving, faster and faster, a mist in the air, piles of snow pushed to the side, the sidewalk grounding my fears. I chew on Rolaids, my stomach clenched like a fist, inhaling exhaust and rotten milk. Coins jingle in a white Styrofoam cup and no I can't spare any change. I open the door to our apartment as slowly and quietly as possible, hoping for a laugh, a gasp, or a moan—anything to show me I am right.

"Hey, honey, I'm making meatloaf. Take off your wet boots and come give me a kiss."

She's happy, her cheeks flushed, and it makes me nervous. When she hugs me at the top of the steps, I hold her tight, and sniff at her head, her hair still damp from a shower. There is no concrete proof, and yet I'm certain she lies to me every day. That or I've lost my mind. She's strayed before, this on again off again thing that we do. But the ring on her finger is a promise—things are supposed to be different now.

I pick at the meal, pushing the food around the plate, and she is nothing but laughter and white teeth. But the mask she wears is one I've seen before, and buried in that sharp, emerald gaze is a glimmer of recognition, a spark of an old lie that she holds close to her chest. I remember passing a man on the sidewalk who was adjusting his tie, a damp negligee at the bottom of our hamper, her workout clothes folded in her gym bag while her body still glistened with sweat. Electricity jumped across my flesh as she darted into the shower and locked the door behind her.

❧

Can you die from a lack of sleep? It turns out you can, and sooner than starvation. It might be a photo finish for me. A lack of sleep can result in many things, so I scan down the list that Google has shown me. Huddled in the dark, sitting at my computer, I peck away at the dirty keys. Sleep is elusive and Candace needs her rest. Irritability: check. Blurred vision: check. Slurred speech: check. Memory lapses: check. Overall confusion: check, check. Hallucinations . . .

I get on the wrong train today in a fog, my thoughts focused on hang-ups, parking stubs and grocery receipts for filet mignon I'm sure I never ate. These are not my people, the usual mix of suits and skirts. The elderly Polish woman sits upright, her hands clenched together, eyes out the window, and her husband—is he already in the ground? An expanse of warehouse juts out to the horizon, concrete bunkers side by side. The boy with the curly dark hair nods to the music, headphones on tight, bass resonating all around him, hidden behind dark sunglasses—is he heading out or coming home? Taut wires bisect the grey sky, as black birds hunch together—harbingers of doom. Doors opening, cars starting, why is this belief in love so easy for others and impossible for me?

Somehow I end up on the wrong METRA rail and wind up in Fox Lake. The first five stops seemed a bit off, not quite the right direction. The names were all a bit foreign to me but I attributed it to a lack of sleep.

Chasing Ghosts

Drifting off between blurry bungalows and strips of warehouses I wake up north of it all. I'm almost in Wisconsin, for Christ's sake. This day is ruined, I've finally lost it, so I call into work, sick. My voice trembles, gravel in my throat. They tell me to take it easy.

The next train heading south isn't for an hour and a tiny diner across the tracks is the only thing open. Wandering over, I soon find myself neck deep in a platter of eggs—bacon grease smeared across my lips and a pot of coffee by my side. The waitress is a stone wall—massive breasts tucked behind a tattered white apron that is splattered with food, her arms spotted with freckles and moles, square jaw tight and unmoving. She shakes her head, clucking into her apron. She's seen my kind before in the dead eyes of her beaten down husband, the daily grind reducing him to pulp. Perhaps her son left home for some tattooed hussy in tight jeans. She's been a witness to things falling apart. Her eyes are on me the entire time I'm there, arms crossed in defiance—waiting for me to reveal myself.

"More coffee?" she asks, her shadow engulfing me.

"I can't control my wife."

She fills up my cup and purses her lips. "And you should? Like a dog maybe, telling her to sit, to stay?"

"No. I just want her to stop fucking other men."

Her eyes go dark, two bits of ore, squinting. "She's missing something, no doubt. What is it you aren't giving her?"

"I wish I knew."

She walks away as dissatisfied as I am. There have been shadows at the periphery today, Candace's ghost tracking me from stop to stop. When I left she was asleep but in that moment before the door clicked shut, while I stood there turning the key, I heard too many things. The sheets were pulled back, the shower turned on, a rumbling in the pipes that shook the whole building and a distant ringing in my head coming from our apartment. She didn't fool me one bit.

I sip at the coffee, and the waitress appears, placing a Danish in front of me. "I didn't order this."

"I know," she says.

"You remind me a lot of my mother," I say, "and I mean that as a compliment."

"I get that a lot," she says. "I guess waiting on you, bringing you something that you didn't ask for, that's enough for you?" she smiles.

"Today, that's all I needed. A bit of kindness." She nods her head once. "Thank you," I say. She shrugs and walks away.

I lean back into the booth, the windows filling up with steam. Outside it could be anything, anywhere—a campus, a hospital, Armageddon.

All day, apparitions have followed me around, an outline of Candace floating in the gray. She is stepping out the front door as my bus heads south. Hopping into a yellow taxi as I descend the steps to the el train below. Skirt lifted, she dashes onto the platform next to mine as my train eases out of the station. There is no answer at home today—no matter what time I call. She is not to be found. Years ago I offered Candace a cell phone and she quickly refused—she wouldn't be tracked like a wild animal.

My cell phone chirps and the ID is blank, unknown

caller it says. I pick it up and she's whispering in my ear. She wants to know where I am.

"Work," I say, and she laughs out loud.

"David, I called the office. They said you were sick. And I'm beginning to agree," she says.

"What do you mean?"

"Your behavior."

"My behavior?" I shout into the phone. I glance around the diner, the waitress pausing with a plate full of bacon and eggs.

"David, perception is reality."

The phone goes quiet and I chew on her words. It doesn't matter what the truth is, that's what she's trying to tell me. If I make it the truth, then whatever I imagine—whatever she believes, it becomes a reality. I'm poisoning the well that we drink from every night. Suddenly, I need to get home.

Candace is waiting for me when I get to the apartment. She is sitting in the living room, a bottle of red wine open on the long, slender table, a glass half full with lipstick dotting the rim. The room is dim behind the floor-to-ceiling drapes, shadows filling every corner.

"We need to talk," she says.

I hang up my coat and sit down.

"I'm not cheating on you, David. I need you to know that."

"What about . . . "

"David," she says, "look at me, look me in the eyes."

I lean forward and her eyes are rimmed with red,

tears held back by mascara and determination, her hands placed gently on my knees.

"I'm not cheating on you," she says.

"Okay," I say. "I hear you. I trust you."

"No, David, you don't," she says, picking up the wine and taking a sip. "And I deserve that. We never talked about what happened . . . "

"Before."

"Before we were married, yes," she says. "And I don't want to dwell on that now. But things aren't right. So I'm giving you three choices, and you have to make one right now."

"Choices, what are you talking about?"

"This is my solution, David."

I pick up her glass of wine, drink it, and fill it again. Candace glances at her watch.

"The phone is going to ring in a couple of minutes. It's the wife of the man I slept with two years ago."

"What the hell, Candace?"

"Just shut up and listen or there's the door." She points.

"Go on," I say.

"This woman is calling me because I left her a message on her cell phone. I've known them both for years now. It's my friend, Melissa."

"Oh my God."

"I can tell her one of three things, and I'm going to leave it up to you, because we either end this game right now and get a divorce, or we find a way to salvage our marriage."

The sunlight is fading, a dull orange glow from the street outside leaking in, but soon we'll be in total darkness.

"I can tell Melissa the truth—that her husband and I had an affair. I can tell her it's still going on. It will end their marriage and she'll put him in the street tonight. I know her. She'll make a pile of his suits out on the sidewalk and set the whole thing on fire."

I laugh, a slow grin easing over my face. The first option has great appeal.

"Two, I can tell Melissa that you and I are in an open relationship and that I'd like for the two of you to have sex."

My mouth opens and I picture Melissa and her hearty laugh, her athletic body tan and fit, my wife's sporty twin—a woman I've quietly lusted after for years. I look at my feet, a heat rushing up the back of my neck.

"She'll do it. I know she's been looking around, unhappy. It'd be our secret—she thinks she can trust me. And she's always liked you."

"Okay, that's an interesting option."

"But, David?"

"Yes?"

"It might be the end of our marriage."

"What do you mean?" I ask.

"Fair or unfair, I don't know if I can handle that. I'm just telling you that now. But at least we'd be even."

It's dark now and I can hardly see her face. But it's better that way.

"What's the third option?" I ask.

"We let it ring. We don't answer it. And you let it all go. No more games, no more accusations from you, no more teasing from me. Enough. We go upstairs and make love and find a way to honor each other. For the first time in a long time, maybe."

I take a breath and rub my temples, my eyes—searching for the ability to let her back in. The phone rings.

THE OFFERING ON THE HILL

I'D BEEN FOLLOWING the train tracks north for three days when I came across the skeletons— a pile of bones in a ring around a cairn of skulls, a bullet hole in the center of each one. The sun beat down on me, one wave of pulsing sunshine after another, my skin like worn leather—my eyes two tiny black dots. One boot followed the other as I pushed onward, faded jeans pasted to my sweaty body like a second layer of skin, a revolver on each hip, leather holsters filled with glistening metal, their weight a comforting presence. I'm too old for this, but the uneasy quiet that has slipped over the land—it is not a death knell—only a beginning. The world has moved on, but my greatest fear is that the dead will never stop laughing.

As hot as it is now, it will be deathly cold tonight, a wave of freezing air washing across the desert as sure as the sickly glowing ball will rise tomorrow. I have to find shelter, or start building a fire soon. In the distance there are mountains, but I can't get there tonight. I don't like the look of the ring, either—the skulls make me uneasy. So it will be baptism by fire—

one dried scrub brush on top of its brother; whatever dead or dying cactus I can find, the rotting boards from an old sign—Death Valley it says, an arrow pointing off in one direction, surely a joke.

When the skulls are covered in debris so that I can't see their gaping mouths any longer, I spark a flame from a wooden match with my thumbnail, and toss it onto the wood. It catches quickly and sends flickering tongues of fire up into the sky as the darkness settles across the land. I raise my head and glance north again, and in the hazy distance the ghost of a train whistle blows sorrow. I walk to the tracks and set my hand upon them—a tiny vibration running through my gnarled fingers, certainly heading away. I've never seen the train going south. No reason to head back that way—nothing but abandoned buildings, rotting car husks, and the stench of the human race gone sour.

So long had I been out in the desert, up in the hills, prospecting and tracking deviant flesh, runaways and bounties hunted with great patience, that there was nothing left for me when I came down—no people, no messages, no television, and no radio—just an endless silence that stretched out into eternity. I'd seen no explosions, nothing nuclear, and the cattle, it could have been anything—starvation, sickness, even poachers—but I gave them a wide berth, anyway.

The only clue I'd found was the word north. Everywhere I went, whispered by the lips of the dead, scratched into pads of paper, and painted on walls— the word north. I found an entire town, Crystal Lake, dry as a bone, the irony not lost on me, with hundreds of cars on the highway pointed in this direction— empty.

THE OFFERING ON THE HILL

None of it made any sense.

But it's where my wife and child may have gone, if they are still alive. The shadows at night creep in and whisper horrible things, violent imagery of my daughter hung up on a cross, wearing a thorny crown, vast pits filled with the walking dead, pillars of fire shooting high into the night.

And then the cold pushes in on me, so I move closer to my pyre. I will slowly rotate as the night goes on, walking around the licking flames, as the freezing wind nips at me, a thin sheet of ice coating my emaciated frame. If I stop moving I will die—the weather shifting to both extremes, blazing hot in the daytime and freezing cold in the night. In the wake of the new world order things had changed. I've been having this dance with the devil for weeks now, and in the morning, when it warms up, I will collapse. For now, it is the gleam in the eyes of my daughter Allie that pushes me on, reminds me why I even bother.

The day I left, her long brown hair was tied back in a ponytail, as a teapot on the stove steamed and whistled—the clocks whirring behind my princess as tears streamed rivulets of dirt down her face. Her mother, Cecilia, God bless her, holding Allie back as her own dark hair fell over her eyes, her face, hiding behind it, unwilling to look at me. I walked out the door, securing our future—and possibly their death.

In the distance I hear wood cracking, splintering, and crashing to the ground—shattering. The thin branches and hollow trunks can't sustain the weight of the ice, and they topple over, ripping up roots, fracturing—turning to shards, fragments, and sparkling dust. Every night I long to walk out into the freezing cold and let the elements take me. But something is calling me north.

⌒

In the morning I come to, lying in the ash around the fire, not burned, but not frozen to death either. A large black bird sits on my feet, tapping its beak on the faded sole of my left boot, yellow sparkling eyes like two marbles rolling around in its feathered, bobbing skull. The beast turns its head to the south, and then leaps into the sky with a rush of foul air, wings spread wide, pushing up into the gray tapestry above us, heading north with a sense of sudden urgency.

The fire pit is just as I had originally found it, a ring of bones around the pile of skulls, no evidence of the fire, no proof that my labor had even happened. I need water soon, so I have to move on.

Three hours later I come to the edge of a forest that squats at the base of an expansive mountain range, sweat running down my neck, my back—dirt and grime slipping down my spine. I can hear the water gurgling, but can't see it yet. My lips crack and bleed, the goatskin at my waist squeezed dry the day before, my eyes on the clouds above, as it grows dark, lightning flashing over the horizon—but the rain, it will never come, not now that I need it. Crashing through the bushes and low-hanging branches, a thin path reveals itself, my feet tripping over roots and buried stones, the sparkle of water glinting through the greenery. I stumble to the pool of water as spider webs stretch across my face, my outstretched hands waving them off, filament in my mouth, a wash of panic mixing with a knot in my gut, the water suddenly my world.

As I kneel at the edge of the creek, by the pool, I cup the cold water and drink, the liquid spilling down my chest. The knees of my jeans soak through with mud, and as I sit up to breathe, gasping, the row of crosses reveals itself to me, on the other side of the oasis. Six, seven of them, all in a row, all shapes and sizes, skeletons strung out and bound with vines, crucified, the nails run through, another row behind them, with nothing but skulls on pikes. Tied around each bit of rotting wood is a single piece of ribbon, each of them a faded pink, moss growing beneath the sacrifices, low white blossoms running off into the woods. I lower the canteen into the cold water, and fill it up, my stomach clenched in knots, my eyes on the whispering leaves—my heart thudding drumbeats in my chest.

It's time to move on.

᎐

I won't be able to make it up the mountain tonight—wouldn't make any sense to get caught out in the open like that, wind and ice spraying certain death. Out of the woods a path deposits me at a tiny shack, a lantern glowing in the window as the sun falls out of the sky. A skeletal dog is tied to the house with an old withered rope, whining and pissing into the dirt as I approach the humble dwelling, the skittish beast eager to say hello.

"It's okay," I say, showing the skinny wreck my open palms. She squats, her tail wagging like a metronome turned all the way up, her eyes glazed over with white, a black lab mix of some sort. She licks my hands, her black muzzle dotted with grey hair, the poor thing dying out here, begging for attention. She must go inside at night, I think to myself, or she'd be frozen to the ground, dead long ago. I run my hands over her ribcage, each bone like a slat of wood, wasting away to nothing. I root around in my gear and bring out a tough stick of jerky, and kneeling in the dry earth I give it to her, and she falls into chewing and licking with a devout worship that makes me a tad bit uneasy.

"Good girl," I say, standing back up.

The door to the structure opens and a grizzled old man peers out, long gray beard hanging down, his eyes the same glossy white as the mutt. In overalls, boots, and a dirty long-sleeved shirt, the man sways in the doorway, a grin slipping over his face.

"That's awfully kind of you, stranger," he says. "Food's hard to come by out this way, and in my condition, our condition, it's difficult to head into town."

I nod my head, realizing he can't see me, and step forward.

"My name's John Ford, and I'm heading north. You seen anyone come by, any sign of life, of late?"

I stand there holding out my hand, the blind coot staring over my shoulder, his whiskers twitching. He extends his gnarled digits to me, and smiles, so I take his hand, like grabbing a fistful of sticks, and shake it.

"Nobody of late. I'm Benjamin Russell, but you can just call me Ben," the old man says. "Come on in, it's gonna get cold soon. Can you bring the dog? She's Jezebel, the old whore, I keep her tied up so she won't wander off, chase after something she shouldn't—but the ice is coming, I'm sure you know all about that."

I turn back to the dog, the meat gobbled up in a frenzy, a rotten sigh coming out of her mouth, death creeping closer every day. And I guess that's a blessing.

"Come on, Jezebel," I mutter, untying the rope from the rusted hook on the post, leading her inside. She knows what's good for her, the cold coming in, so she obliges.

Inside it's warm, a potbelly stove glowing in the corner. Not much to see in here, a tiny bed to one side, the stove, a small wooden table with two rickety old chairs, and a few pots and pans for cooking. Along the inside of one wall, just under the only window is a stack of wood—plenty it looks like for the night, for days in fact, possibly weeks.

"You found the creek, I imagine," he says, sitting down in one of the chairs. "So you're set on water. I head down every couple of days to fill up some jugs, got the path memorized, nothing much to trip over out this way. We got a few sacks of beans and rice, it's not much, but you're welcome to join us for dinner."

"Don't mind if I do," I say, plopping into the other chair.

"Got a few extra blankets and the floor, that's about it, my friend. Unless you want my bed, I don't think I could keep you from taking it."

"That's fine, Ben. The floor is just fine."

The old man gets up and walks to the bag of dried beans, and then the rice, taking a few scoops from each burlap sack with a tin cup, depositing it all in a cast iron Dutch oven. He lifts a jug off the table, adding in some water, and then reaches for some dried herbs in a small wooden bowl, sprinkling them into the pot. He sits back down, tired and bent.

"You headed over the mountain, John? North?" the man asks.

"I reckon. That's the way the wind is pulling me, hoping to find my family, my wife and daughter. I'm hoping they followed the same signs I've been reading for weeks. Guess I'll see what's left in a world that's suddenly gone dark—what's on the other side."

The man nods.

"Take some of the feed with you, if you want, son— Jezebel and I aren't long for this world. I got a couple bullets with our names on them, if it comes to that, or we might just wink out in the same long, dark night. Who knows?"

"Thanks," I mutter. "I'll take you up on that offer."

The dog sits next to the stove, still shivering now and then, her body doing its best to digest the jerky, something she probably hasn't eaten in months.

"Have you seen many people since it all went quiet, get much company?" I ask.

The wind picks up, the cold beating against the shack, and I'm grateful to be inside. I can feel the ice slipping through the cracks in the wood, nipping at my exposed flesh, but I suppose the structure will hold.

He sighs, his white orbs open wide, trying to remember.

"There was one day, we got a whole mess of folks, a long line of feet moving over the dirt. I could hear them coming, like a stampede, and I went to the door and stood there, I listened. Both of us did. I heard a few greetings, but mostly it was quiet, eerie almost, must have been a couple dozen people drifting by,

The Offering on the Hill

hardly a word, nobody stopping, just the creaking of bodies, the sighs and moans, a few kids crying, a sharp word here and there, but I don't know if your wife and child were in there. Maybe. You never know."

I nod and take a breath.

"You been over?" I ask.

"The mountain?" he replies. "Long time ago. It's a bitch, you'll cross a few streams, so water's not the problem. Cold, of course, a few wild things up in the rocks, the scraggly woods that are dying all up and down the hill, coyotes, snakes, the usual."

I nod my head.

"And . . . "

He opens his mouth as the wind kicks up again, the shack rattling and shaking, the smell of the beans and rice simmering, drifting to me, my stomach clenching and unclenching in hunger.

"What?" I ask.

He smiles, his mouth a mess, gums bleeding over his yellow teeth, wiping his face with a shaky hand, his eyes blinking and twitching.

"Nothing," he says, as the window rattles.

He stands and walks to the stove, the skillet bubbling, stirring with an old wooden spoon, mumbling to himself, rubbing his lower back, the dog lifting her head, whimpering.

"I don't know if they all made it over," is what the old man says, and I swear he's crying, his back to me, but it's getting dark, and I can't see his face.

The dog sits up and stares at the man, whining, a low growl deep in her belly.

"Shut up, Jezebel," the man yells suddenly, turning

around, his pale skin flushed. "If I want to tell him, I'll tell him."

She lies back down, quiet now, cloudy eyes darting back and forth from the sound of her master's voice, to me, and then she closes them, surrendering.

"I don't know if any of them made it over, son, is what I'm trying to say."

"What do you mean?" I ask.

He rubs his face and sits back down, tears running down his wrinkled skin.

"Out here it's every man for himself, right?" he says. "I guess I could have said no, and let him take me, just surrender. Not like I'm living like a king out here. The fucking thing could have stayed up there, gotten what came its way, I don't know why it had to offer me anything."

"What are you talking about, Ben? Who is up in the hills? Is somebody bothering you? Want me to go talk to them, put a scare in them? I don't mind."

Ben cackles and rubs his white eyes, shaking—his mouth hanging loose, lips trembling.

"I wish it was that simple, John. A long time ago before this darkness fell over the land, I made a deal. I can't say I believed much of it at the time, I was sick with the cancer, dying, and felt like I might like to live a little longer, not die out here in the silence, alone. He showed me a path, the new path that goes over the mountain, one he'd been clearing for a long time, months I suspect. Just send them this way, he said. And then he put his hands on my head, and laid me

THE OFFERING ON THE HILL

down on the bed, running his long fingers over my flesh, kneading here and there, pushing his fingers in, the pain, the tenderness, he knew what he was doing. There was no blood, but the cancer went away. He ran his hands over my skull, and the headaches stopped. Held my hands and knelt beside my bed, and the arthritis disappeared."

I nod my head, listening, as the wind beats the shack and the boards rustle, dust and cold air filling the space.

"In a moment of weakness, I said okay. And then he left. Now and then he would come down out of the mountain and palaver, always in a slightly different shape. Once, as the echo of my long dead father, once as a gangly shadow of my childhood best friend, and once as a younger version of myself, still handsome and stout. I was drinking a lot then. He'd leave me a jug, and I'd suck it dry. The black bird would soar over, before I lost my sight, and soon enough Jezebel arrived on my doorstep, to keep me company, and not long after, Rebecca—my wife."

I take a breath and don't say a word.

"Not always my wife, not some long lost love come back to me, no, not from the grave or anywhere else— something new, something I never had, and we lived a simple life. I never asked how or why she was here, I just accepted her, as one might take a coin, a gold watch, a gift on an anniversary, or holiday, perhaps. Long black hair and dark eyes, pale skin, she was a fallen angel that had no business being here. No children, no, we didn't allow that. I didn't. Not that we didn't couple, but she would never birth an abomination, nothing that the dark one sent me could

-199-

be continued, you understand?" he asks, staring at me, eyes blind and casting out into the darkness, searching for forgiveness. "There are ways to end beginnings, and several times I did exactly that."

"Ben . . . " I say, even though I struggle to believe.

"Let me finish," he says. "She died many years ago—I stopped counting at some point. Not sure exactly how old I am, Jezebel defying the odds right with me, one hundred, two hundred. I don't know."

I squint at him. The liar, he's lost his goddamned mind.

"I supposed in the end she was just curious, Rebecca, following the path too far, my warnings falling on deaf ears, her laughter at such imaginings simply contempt for my rotten heart, and my empty head. I guess I could have just said coyote, and left it at that, if not for the necklace. He brought me her locket one day, coming down from the hills in the form of a sick, brown bear. Lumbering down, sending the dog into a fit, dropping the jewelry in the dirt, knowing I was watching, its open mouth a black hole—rotting, buzzing, a low growl slipping out into the air."

Stories, the old man is telling me stories, just to pass the time, I think.

"It preys on your fears, John, whatever you long for, whatever you miss—this is what it will become for you. I warn you now, so that maybe you can make it over, outwit the demon, and pass by unobstructed. It was my father, who never held me once, the word love never slipping past his lips; it was my best friend, acts of betrayal, a sneer on his face as he took so many things that were mine; and even my younger self, what I might have been, if only I'd tried harder, if only I'd listened."

THE OFFERING ON THE HILL

Outside the wind picks up, shaking the shack again, the ice pelting the side of the structure, the window rattling in its frame.

"That's quite a story, Ben," I say.

He frowns at me and stands.

"Dinner's ready," he grumbles, spooning the beans and rice into a wooden bowl, handing me a bent silver spoon. "Eat up, son. Tomorrow, you'll need your strength."

$\backsim$

When the sun rises the next morning my head is filled with the echo of animals howling under a moonlit sky, the scratching of Jezebel's nails on the plank floor, in her own fitful dream, hunter or hunted—not sure which. Ben sits on the edge of his bed staring at me, his jaw clenching and unclenching—staring as if he still had eyes that worked, staring out into all of our futures.

I sit up.

"You okay, Ben," I ask, rubbing my face, pain running up and down my spine, my hands icy cold and partially numb, the potbelly stove down to a dull glow.

"I don't expect you to believe it all," he says. "I know how it sounds. I wish there was some way to convince you of the truth."

I wave him off, and then realize he can't see my hand.

"It doesn't matter, Ben, if it happened or didn't happened, I'm heading over the mountain. If I see your buddy, I'll put in a good word for you, okay?"

The old coot laughs and smiles.

-201-

"You really don't understand, my friend," he says, standing up.

He walks to the stove, and with a pair of old leather gloves, opens the front of the metal beast. He grabs a few logs from the stack against the wall, and tosses them in, shutting the door with his knee.

"I'll put on some coffee," he says, shuffling over to the bags of supplies in the corner, "you need to get on your way. If you hurry, you can make it up and over and down again, about ten miles total, just under five thousand feet in elevation, I reckon."

We don't talk much over the coffee, beans ground by hand, Jezebel sitting by my side, resting her nose upon my lap. I eat the rest of the rice and beans from the night before, warmed up, sticking to my ribs, as Ben watches, clasping his hands. When I take a step outside to piss, the heat is already sliding over the hillside. Ben fixes me a pack with a small metal pot, and several cups of his supplies.

When he steps outside, I can tell he's upset, but he won't talk about it, shuffling his feet, the dog sitting beside him.

"Here," he says, handing me the sack. "This should help you get over, whatever is left on the other side. You won't die of starvation today; I can at least do that much."

"I appreciate it, Ben," I say, and I hand him a few sticks of jerky. "Save it for the mutt for later, and have yourself a chaw if it won't rip your rotten old teeth out."

He grins and takes it, and then holds out his hand.

"Good luck, John," he says, his white glassy eyes trembling in his head. What does he see right now, I wonder—the past, the present, or the future?

Or maybe nothing at all.

"Thanks," I mutter, shaking his hand.

I bend down to pet the dog, and she licks my hand, the gesture rippling over my flesh, triggering memories from days gone by, back when things were domesticated, when the world hadn't already run its course. I choke back a muffled sob and swallow hard, clearing my throat.

"I better get going. I'll keep an eye out for both man and beast, Ben, I promise."

He nods his head, and I set off up the path he warned me about, the only obvious trail over the mountain, to whatever family I might have left. The sign at the edge of the worn out dirt trail is pounded into the dry soil, crooked and faded, the word north painted on it in shaky letters, as if written with a finger, something a child might do, an arrow pointing to the left. The letters are in a faded red paint, or perhaps something else, and as I look up to the clear blue sky, the black bird circles, and then disappears over the woods.

Before I disappear around a bend, into the thin pines and maples that rest at the base of the hill, I turn to wave at them both, forgetting one last time that they can't see a damn thing. I wave anyway, feeling like I could have done more, said something—not been so ornery and doubtful. What's done is done, and I wave at them anyway, and as I head up the mountain the dog barks once, wagging its tail, and as the darkness swallows me up, Ben waves back.

෴

For three hours I work my way up the hill, stopping only to refill my water whenever I pass over a creek or stream. Though it gets cooler the higher I go, the sun slowly rises, the woods warming around me, insects chirping, a red-tailed hawk gliding over an opening in the canopy, sailing on the thermals that push around the mountain range.

When I stop to rest for a bit, sitting on a fallen oak, pulling off my left boot to root out a rock, a mangy smell drifts toward me, and I look up and around, eyes on the path, and then to the woods. Something rotten, and dirty—not sure what it is. I slip my boot back on and stand up, leaving the bag of supplies on the ground, both hands to my hips, holsters unsnapped.

I sniff again. Something isn't right. There's a wet smell, something gone sour, flesh baking in the sun, feces and urine, a heavy odor filling the air. The woods are silent, not a bluebird or jackdaw to be heard, just the thudding of my heart and my own shallow breath.

Down the path saunters an aging coyote, with long ambling legs, yellow eyes, its fur torn in patches, faded brown and grey, one ear missing a chip. When I hear a panting behind me, I look back down the other way, and see another one coming up the hill. And from out of the bushes, two more from the left, starting to snarl now, two more from the right. They are skinny, with their mouths open, yapping at each other, so I move to the center of the path, guns pulled out now, my head on a swivel, back and forth. The leader stops at the top of the trail and sits down, panting, as his brothers close rank. I cock the hammer on the right pistol, and then the left, the creatures never slowing their pace, happy with their numbers, starting to slink low, ears up high.

The Offering on the Hill

I wait for one to leap, contemplating a shot at the leader, hoping it might make them scatter, counting in my head the number of bullets, wondering if I'm a good enough shot.

To the right, and up the hill there is a great ripping sound from deep in the woods, as if a tree has been uprooted, leaves rushing by, and then a heavy thud, as it crashes to the forest floor, and the animals flee in all directions, gone in the blink of an eye.

Bear?

It moves closer, and I can see the tops of the trees swaying back and forth, suddenly the forest full of life, all manner of bird cawing and chirping, a flutter of wings, a jackrabbit shooting past me, and I almost pull the trigger, cursing the long-eared bastard. Bushes rustle and I can see it moving closer to the path, just up a little bit, branches snapping, twigs cracking, and then the foliage parts, and out the creature steps onto the trail.

I stare in wonder, and suddenly think that maybe Ben wasn't lying at all.

The boy stands there in torn pants, tied with a rope, no shoes, and no shirt, his head shaved, eyes brown and pooling. His feet are so filthy that the toes almost look bonded together into one cloven hoof.

"Are you heading over the mountain?" he asks. I open my mouth to speak, but nothing comes out. He holds his hands in front of his distended belly, scratches and bruises up and down his arms, a smile filling his face; too wide—far too wide.

"That was the plan," I muster.

"Did Ben send you my way?" he asks, just a child, maybe ten or twelve, something not right, and if I turn

-205-

my head to one side and squint, he looks so very familiar.

"In a manner of speaking, I guess he did," I exhale.

"You can put those away," he says.

I look down, and the guns are holstered.

"Have others been by?" I ask, "since things, well . . . "

"Since the end times began?" he asks.

"Recently. My wife, my daughter . . . "

And at this he grins again, his teeth not yellow, but sparking white, from this distance not square and humble, but slightly filed, as if to a point.

"This is my mountain now," he says, not moving, eyes blinking.

"Look, son, I'm just trying to get over and down, won't be on your mountain hardly any time at all."

"I'm afraid that's not good enough," he says. "There must be a tribute, and there is none that I can see. Are you not willing to make an offering?" he asks. "What exactly do you have to offer?" he asks, eyebrows furrowing, a frown sliding his face down, his mouth shut, as the sun settles behind rapidly moving clouds, the forest dimming, the air turning cooler—goose bumps running across my flesh.

He takes a step toward me and I pull the pistols and fire.

He laughs.

Looking down, my fists are held in front of me, my index fingers pointed out in his direction, thumbs cocked up.

Empty.

"No, my friend," he says. "Not what I was looking for, I'm afraid."

And in the distance there is a single gunshot, a

crack, loud and clear, and the boy looks down the hill toward where the shack must still stand, his face tightening and flushing red. I take a breath, and a second shot startles the air, a colony of bats escaping from two large, grey boulders to our right, from a deep slash in the earth, running off into the sky, as raindrops pelt the top of the forest.

I stare at this boy, my hands open now, out in front of me, as if holding him back by sheer will.

He walks closer and I cannot move, the boy up close, reaching into his dingy pants, pulling out a pocket knife, flipping it open, running the blade over the palm of his left hand. And then again, completing an "x." He reaches up and I find myself bending over, while inside I scream no and run and godinheaven, but I cannot refuse him. He places his spread hand on my forehead, leaving a sticky red handprint, and then he steps away.

"You may pass," he says, exhaling.

And for a moment I am a child again, scratching at my shaved head, the lice captured in a comb, their little legs scurrying about, the sink filled with hair, a trickle of blood, one nick of my head, the boy some distant echo, rippling out in time, a mirror image of what I once was. Turning back a single time, eyes squinting, he slips into the woods again, the crashing of bushes flattened, the creak and groan of a massive oak tipping down the hill, snapping off branches, and slamming to the earth.

And then quiet.

What lies on the other side of the mountain?

I fear there is nothing left at all, just empty wishes and dirt.

RICHARD THOMAS

⸺

I spend the rest of the day in a hot daze working my way to the top of the mountain, pushing on, eager to make the top, so I can rest for a moment and gather my thoughts. Along the way, there are many signs that life and death have both come this way.

After leaving the boy, I find an old, dead scrub oak, with nothing but empty branches, a long dark scar running down one side, as if struck by lightning, the grass around it burnt and flat. In the dry branches are pairs of shoes, tied together—swinging in the breeze. There are tiny white baby booties, small tennis shoes, hiking boots, anything with laces, suspended in the air, dark fruit that will never blossom. At the base of the tree are dozens of cowboy boots, sandals and anything without a lace—without the ability to hang. Perhaps not all made an offering here, these shoes remnants of their previous lives, their bones scattered up and down the hill, altars made from their empty skulls; perhaps some made it over this hill.

I move on.

An hour later I stumble across a small pit just off the path to the left, and for a moment I think it is filled with writhing snakes. But as the sun glints through the leaves, and the branches sway, the hole is illuminated in flashes of light, something sparkling in it, a hint of metal, and then I realize what it is. At the bottom of this hole are hundreds of belts, the metal catching light now and then, intertwined black and brown, woven hemp, not moving at all, just a trick upon my eyes.

I keep moving.

-208-

The Offering on the Hill

Finally, I reach the top of the mountain, the open space covered in rock and shale, a few scraggly pines and low bushes, the sky clear for miles in every direction. I can see the train tracks running north and south, but no sign of the great metal beast. I can see the tiny shack where Ben shared a meal with me, and the sterile desert to the south. And to the north, I can see open land, green grass and widespread growth, a whisper of smoke drifting up into the sky, and what looks to be a settlement of sorts, a few small buildings, too far to see any movement, but a sign of life, at least.

There is hope.

I take a moment to chew on the last of the jerky, to drink my water, and to prepare myself for what lies in wait. I had come to expect nothing, just the dust and dirt, a few remnants perhaps, ready to find only an echo of what had been before. Some must have made it over, a few at least, or perhaps they were from the other side, not making the journey south, aware of what lurks in the hills.

I head down.

The day slips past, hours unfolding one after the other, sweat coating my body, the sun dipping down over the horizon, and before it disappears, I emerge from the woods, making it to the flat lands, the path continuing on, right up to a few dilapidated buildings.

Tents, teepees, and lean-tos are scattered around a few small cabins, most of them much like Ben's, barely standing, cut from the woods around us, built by hand many years ago, faded and worn, but still upright. One larger structure looks as if it has been built in the past year, new wood, the cuts still fresh, the chimney spilling smoke into the air. In the middle of the grounds is a large fire pit, ringed with grey and white rocks, black ash filling the center, a boy and girl snapping branches, filling up the circle with dry wood, heading back and forth to the woods. The girl turns to me, drops the wood and lets out a scream.

"Daddy!" she yells, and I drop my sack, my eyes beginning to water, as she flies to me, my Allie, dirty and smudged, a small red handprint on her forehead. I kneel in the dirt as she crashes into me, and I hold her, crying now, a great weight fluttering off into the sky.

"How did you get over?" she asks, pulling back, looking at me, as my eyes run over her. She looks healthy, happy even, tears running down her dusty face.

"I imagine much like you all did," I said.

"I knew you'd come, I knew you'd make it," she says.

I take a deep, uncertain breath.

"Are you okay?" I ask.

She nods.

"Where's your mother?" I ask, and her eyes go dark, her head dipping.

Out of the structures, the main house, and the woods, more children emerge. They are all ages, all races, much like Allie—slightly dirty and dusty, some cuts and scratches, but not sickly, not dying, their arms filled with wood, or jugs of water, some carrying baskets with potatoes, carrots, and onions. They all wander over, their eyes wide, smiles slipping across their faces. On each of their foreheads is a singular, red blotch, some faded, some fresher, but all still remaining, not washed away, not erased. These handprints that were left in blood, the tributes have not been forgotten.

A boy and girl emerge from the main house, older, but not much more than eighteen. They look tired, the girl holding an infant in her arms, the boy grasping her arm as they approach. They must be in charge.

"This is my father," Allie says, walking toward them.

I hold out my hand, and the boy shakes it, the girl smiling, whispering to her baby, as she bounces it up and down.

"Is this it?" I ask. "Where's your mother, Allie, the other parents?"

I look around at the children, the red marks on their foreheads, and I understand.

"She's not here, Daddy," Allie says, walking back to me, grasping my hand. "There was a price to pay, the offering on the hill."

The boy nods his head and speaks up. "There were choices to be made," he says, "And our parents made them. The way of the old world is gone, destroyed," he says. "This is a new beginning, a second chance."

I take a breath, and hold my daughter's hand. I look into the faces of the children, the way they stand close to one another, the wood, the water, the food—united in their efforts, the echo of their parents' sacrifice branded on their skin.

"Do you have room for one more?" I ask.

The boy looks at my forehead, the red stamp, down at my daughter, and laughs.

"Of course we have room," he says. "We're working on the fire right now," he says. "Gets cold around here at night," he chuckles, "as I'm sure you know. Not as bad as the other side, but still—pretty frigid. Come rest by the ring, catch up with your daughter, we have water, food—come, sit. It'll be dark soon."

Allie leads me by the hand toward the bonfire, and the children follow us, laughing and asking questions, their hands on me, just a little touch here and there, making sure I'm real, something new, something familiar, and then they disperse into the woods, back to work. I am an exciting part of their day, but they know what comes at night, and to survive, there must be fire, there must be heat. We sit and talk, unable to release each other, holding hands, her climbing into my lap. Beyond the houses crops grow, the dead desert south of us gone, the fertile soil here ripe for growth, no nuclear winter, no death and disease, the mountain, perhaps, separating the living from the dead. I don't think too hard about it—I simply hold my daughter, and breathe.

ABOUT THE AUTHOR

Richard Thomas is the author of six books—*Disintegration* and *Breaker* (Random House Alibi), *Transubstantiate* (Otherworld Publications); two short story collections, *Staring Into the Abyss* (Kraken Press) and *Herniated Roots* (Snubnose Press); and one novella of *The Soul Standard* (Dzanc Books). With over 100 stories published, his credits include *Cemetery Dance, PANK, Gargoyle, Weird Fiction Review, Midwestern Gothic, Arcadia, storySouth, Qualia Nous, Chiral Mad 2 & 3, Gutted* and *Shivers VI*. He has won contests at ChiZine and One Buck Horror, and has received five Pushcart Prize nominations to date. He is also the editor of four anthologies: *The New Black* and *Exigencies* (Dark House Press), *The Lineup: 20 Provocative Women Writers* (Black Lawrence Press) and *Burnt Tongues* (Medallion Press) with Chuck Palahniuk and Dennis Widmyer. In his spare time, he is a columnist and teacher at LitReactor, an instructor at the University of Iowa Summer Writing Festival, and Editor-in-Chief at Dark House Press. His agent is Paula Munier at Talcott Notch. For more information, visit www.whatdoesnotkillme.com.

If you enjoyed this book, be sure to check out other Crystal Lake Publishing books for your Dark Fiction, Horror, Suspense, and Thriller needs.

We hope you enjoyed this title. If so, we'd be grateful if you could leave a review on your blog or any of the other websites and outlets open to book reviews. Reviews are like gold to writers and publishers, since word-of-mouth is and will always be the best way to market a great book. And remember to keep an eye out for more of our books.

Connect with Crystal Lake Publishing

Website (be sure to sign up for our newsletter):
www.crystallakepub.com

Facebook:
www.facebook.com/Crystallakepublishing

Twitter:
https://twitter.com/crystallakepub

With unmatched success since 2012, Crystal Lake Publishing has quickly become one of the world's leading indie publishers of Mystery, Thriller, and Suspense books with a Dark Fiction edge.

Crystal Lake Publishing puts integrity, honor, and respect at the forefront of our operations.

We strive for each book and outreach program that's launched to not only entertain and touch or comment on issues that affect our readers, but also to strengthen and support the Dark Fiction field and its authors.

Not only do we publish authors who are destined to be legends in the field (and as hardworking as us), but we also look for men and women who care about their readers and fellow human beings. We only publish the very best Dark Fiction and look forward to launching many new careers.

We strive to know each and every one of our readers, while building personal relationships with our authors, reviewers, bloggers, pod-casters, bookstores and libraries.

Crystal Lake Publishing is and will always be a beacon of what passion and dedication, combined with overwhelming teamwork and respect, can accomplish: unique fiction you can't find anywhere else.

We do not just publish books, we present you worlds within your world, doors within your mind, from talented authors who sacrifice so much for a moment of your time.

This is what we believe in. What we stand for. This will be our legacy.

Welcome to Crystal Lake Publishing.

We hope you enjoyed this title. If so, we'd be grateful if you could leave a review on your blog or any of the other websites and outlets open to book reviews. Reviews are like gold to writers and publishers, since word-of-mouth is and will always be the best way to market a great book. And remember to keep an eye out for more of our books.

THANK YOU FOR PURCHASING THIS BOOK

CPSIA information can be obtained at www.ICGtesting.com
Printed in the USA
BVOW06s2145040516

446841BV00028B/173/P